Somethingness

ROHN ENGH

drawings by the author

CONTENTS

THE MUSIC   Part 9

"Our lives teach us who we are."
~ Salman Rushdie

WE HUMANS

SOMETHINGNESS

As we grow now together
We grow now further away.
The you that I know
Is becoming vast, as endless
As God's infinity.
I love you. I hate you.
And in a starflash I do neither.
I float in the cosmic nothingness
Grasping for something of you.
Give me love or hate,
I'll cherish either,
But I plead, give me somethingness
Of you.

A DECEMBER WALK TO THE BEACH

From the Midwest winter spoils I come
To this end of the rumpled road East
Where I can look to the horizon division
And see no tree no mountains no fence.
This nothingness extends to infinity,
Where hidden tales ferment, of old
And chronicled mariners of foreign stripes,
Of children and elderly, perishing distress,
Lying in wet coffins unprotected from curious urchins.
Where revolving motions of sneering waves
Lap at my absurd Midwest boots that
Leave foreign dents in the auburn sand,
While spider-like creatures snap at my heels.
The wretched wind sings asynchronous tunes
To seduce me to come East into its jowls
And be enveloped by the harsh cold sea of blue
Made of eons of mineral particles and raging rain
Sucked from innocent clouds that damage
And tear fragile dreams and unkempt lives
Into washed-up residue
On cold hard vacant days of December.

NOTHING WORDS

In the Grande Cauldron of oral jewels and marbles
Dwells a stormy selection we call words:
Unmoving, even silent, unless we put them in motion,
Stir them, fashion them, pet them.
They are fingerprints awaiting our expression.

Blindly we pluck them out
And begin their careless worldly relationships,
As fragile and varied as the phrases
From where they are molded.
In their absence we have a nothingness.

These jewels and marbles
From the music of our life experience,
We dabble with them and gamble,
Testing our untried confidence,
Knowing there is no warranty for their misuse.
Something should be said for words unsaid.

UNCLE BILL

Now there was Uncle Bill,
He was quiet as a mouse.
The thing I liked about him best...
If he were coming to visit,
We didn't have to clean the house.

NOTHINGNESS

As a youngster I had seen the road sign often,
Behind the overgrown brush.
A road sign that posted, "Bessemer 4 miles."
It was a dirt road, as most were in those days.
It passed beyond a distant oak,
And to the next farm house, connected by phone lines
That followed the curvature of the rolling hills
To another distant farm house,
That followed the curvature of the earth.

Except for the mailman and school bus
The road seldom knew traffic.
Nothing to divulge, nothing to learn from this road.
Only commonplace farms and fence lines
Separated by a herd of cows and a tree row
Planted generations earlier.
So I never drove this road of no mystery
When I got my first teenage automobile
After high school graduation.

And then I left town.
And have spent 25 years in the City.
Oddly, I thought of that road sometimes.
Maybe because it reflected the nothingness
I was experiencing at my unimportant job.
A road that went nowhere
And one I knew nothing about
And never intended to visit.
A landscape illusion
That no artist would be inspired to render.

Today, at my 25th class reunion,
I am back in my village with a few hours to spare,
Scribbling these lines in the wooden booth
At Rayne's Grill and Dance Pavillion.
Before I return to the distant airport in my rented car,
And I am enticed to visit this road.
I wonder if it has experienced change
(Like my prospering classmates)
Or does it remain steadfast
In its nothingness?

SWEET SIXTEEN

At age sixteen I gave myself a gift
That has lasted me a lifetime
Still with me when I need a lift
Now no longer in my springtime.

This gift would always help me out
When winter came upon me.
My gift would see me through a drought
And return me to my harmony.

Life has its way of making us
Conform to basic routine,
Most grownups label life so tedious
My gift was to stay a teen.

You could say I lived a double life
With private world between.
Although I'm proud to be a grown-up wife
I continue to stay sixteen.

My appearance betrays that I am not
An innocent colleen.
But with the gift that I have got,
I still think I'm a teen.

Time's gone fast these eighty years,
My life has been serene.
I'm not fearful as eternity nears,
Since I am still sixteen.

THE NOTICER

Let the massive, swarming parade of humanity
Pass on by with their dreary insanity,
And let me choose that individual, proud,
Who walks in strength above the crowd.

I speak of the person, who shows nobility,
Who enters our confluence with capability.
It's the "Noticer" I speak of here,
Who listens to others with attentive ear.

Like a feline presence, still and serene,
The Noticer absorbs and is seldom seen.
Not one to hover or stare down its prey,
But stays to the side in a delicate way.

The Noticer sees with discerning eye
The common frailties of you and I.
Quick of mind and with sensitive speed
The Noticer is aware of human need.

Acting with respect and avoiding violence.
The Noticer thrives in discreet silence,
And you will observe that this rare creature
Reigns supreme as both student and teacher.

In dull human beings it's absence of notice,
That you soon recognize in those who don't focus.
The world is burdened with this human freight
Of non-noticing people, who we scramble to escape.

THRIFTY SHOPPING

To most, it's always been a mystery
At a neighborhood flea market sale.
You're always bound to see a she
But you rarely ever see a male.

The puzzle can be swiftly solved
If you look at it this way:
To let decisions be resolved
Just give the she her way.

The art of haggling at a sale
Does not require a patent.
Just don't leave shopping to a male
A woman's the better combatant.

PLAIN AIR

This is a nothing time for me.
The air that I own I share with others.
Not neighbors nor a nearby passersby
But persons far away
Unbeknownst to me,
The faraway passersby.

This nothing air is dispatched
Much like music sounds or radio waves
And as much, is sightless
But full of meaningful letters and sounds.
Air does have sounds, though it is nothing.
Like the nothing I feel today.

10TH INNING

Must have gone home
And I'm alone
In this near vacant stadium
This cemetery.
Watching the players
Perform as they have
For years and years and years.

The rulebook said nine innings
But if the game lasts longer
We can stay 'til it's done.
Our ticket says so.

The boisterous woman,
The brawny man with the hat,
The child who fell asleep,
The serious lady executive,
The electronic teen,
The secretary who read a
    newspaper,
And Joe of Joe's Repair
(It said so on his blue jacket).
They've all left...
Gone. It's a catacomb now.

They left before it was over.
And with them humankind.
The noise they make, the odors,
"S'cuse me, may I get through?"
Above the sound of the speaker.
Turn the volume down.
No need to shout so, now.
It's a graveyard here.

Oh, well.
The team will be back
Tomorrow night.
Won't they?
Does the sun come up?

I see a familiar lone face
Over there
In aisle 9 row 32.
No. It's not him.
Or it might be.
My eyes are getting bad.

I wasn't prepared for this.
To be the last one out.
To cheer vacantly alone.
A non-enjoy of victory.

PARTY

He was not much bigger than my brother
Who is 5' 10" and 3/4".
He walked by me and nodded,
Not close enough to rub my shoulder
But close enough for others
At this after-the-game beer party
To notice that he noticed me.

He was from Avery, my hometown
And had played football with my brother
On the varsity, for three years.
And now he was a wide-receiver at State.
Others could see he nodded to me.
It was a genuine smile, I thought.
And I suppose others did too.

The beer tasted good that evening.
The girls were friendly.
We all stayed crowded in that large room
And made significant noise
And he stayed with us.
I think he left about midnight
And that's when the party shut down.

CLEAN

In late autumn before the first snowfall, the county officials have permissioned me, to burn the accumulated fence posts and other farm and home residue dumped in the back 40 clearing.

Wearing my Mackinaw jacket and husband's day-glow hunting cap, I light that first portion of dried leaves and straw and heaped-up memorabilia and watch, yes, along with the ancestors,
the blaze announce to the skies that Ritual Combustion has begun.

I toss in gnarled windfall branches and frosty rotted shed siding and page after typewritten page harvested from the last century's files, and other memories that deserve to waft to the sky as gray particles. The bonfire fingers shoot higher than my head and I use tools to tend the blaze that eventually simmers to a glow, swirling its soot and creosote into my face and clothing.

I brush harmless cinders from my shoulders and sweep powdered grime from my ringlets and fine ash from my eyelashes. Miniature charcoal crumbs tumble into my ears and a film of smoke envelopes my eyeballs.

As I stoke the remaining embers the swirling aroma from disintegrated matter crawls into my clothing secretly. The organic fire-fermented mash that I create by the final water splashes on the remaining coals at sundown, sneer and simmer in the stingy evening light..

The promise of a clean shower to scour the carbon flavor from my body occupies my mind as I head back to home to the metal knobs and plastic lining of our upstairs shower stall. I test the temperature and slip into the stream of H2 O, the counterpoint to fire. I let the shower rain beat against me, forming a dark whirlpool in the plastic basin rushing down the silver drain to rebirth -- returned to the soil like liquid dust.

I soap my hair and re-scent it and scrub my toes and heels and clean and wash all my body parts inside and out, up and down. Ah! Clean as a whistle, or a baby's bottom, or the hound's tooth or the breeze. Clean, clean, makes all that was -- seem successfully done and buried.

I emerge from the shower with a white towel saying goodbye to uncleanliness. I brush my teeth and tongue. I dress in my winter pajamas and sit down, with a book, once more in my rocking chair by, --yes... the fireside.

DIFFERENT

You are different
Your blood, your mind
Your tears, your eyes
Your sweat and brow.
You cannot accept
Our ordinariness.

You are different.
Even a child knows it
Or a dog or a cat.
And you walk with pride
Knowing
That you cannot accept
The ordinariness of us.
We pedestrians
Who should respect you
With awe and reverence.

We, without aspirations
Or commendable thoughts.
We look at you,
And walk momentarily
With you
But soon fall behind.

VOYEUR

In the fifth floor of my building, lights out,
I'm standing in darkness, watching on a winter night,
The silhouetted figure is moving,
Directly across, over there on the other fifth floor.

The four windows of the apartment are spread out
Like four squares of a newspaper cartoon,
The figure moving in and out of each square.
Doing this and that. Unaware.

Changing directions like a wind-up toy,
It is moving from room to room,
Putting this here, taking that from there,
Pausing now and then, contemplating?

I think it is a man; no it is a woman,
It is moving, always intent, figuring, thinking,
Moving productively from room to room.
The mystery of it all. Very intense.

It pauses and seems to look my way.
I step behind my curtain.
Who is this person?
Is it now my turn?

TRAIN TALK

The businessman on the commuter train
Sitting next to the window
Said to the man beside him,
"I wish I lived in a small town
Where there are no streetlights,
Freeways, and rush hour traffic.
That man said, "I live in a small town
And I wish I lived on a farm
Where I could wake up each day
To clean air and quietude."
The man across the aisle said,
"I live on a farm and my wish is
To live in an undeveloped country
Where there are no taxes
And government regulations.
The man next to him by the window
Said smiling, "I just arrived
From a third world country
And I am eager to live
In the city we are all travelling to."

MY FACE

I have a mask hanging on a hook by my door.
It looks like a hockey protection mask - pure white,
No expression, no indication of what the wearer is thinking.
When I go out to my business day, I put it on.
It hides my glances and my grimaces
When I deal at my office, or on the street or
    at the pharmacy.
Or with waiters, or telemarketers, or salesmen,
    or my customers.

In the evening, when I arrive home
I replace my mask with another mask.
It is also pure white but the expression is pleasant,
    slightly smiling.
And it serves well when I'm helping with the meal,
The homework, or the dishes, or the laundry,
Or finding the remote.

When the newspapers have all been folded for
    re-cycling
And the house lights and the TV turned off
And the dog fed and the cat put out
And the to-do list on the frig crossed off
And tomorrow's soccer game noted on the calendar,
And teeth brushed,
I recall that I have a wife
And enter our bedroom maskless.

BEING ALONE IS NOT LONELINESS

You can find me in my studio.
"It's my favorite place",
I tell my intellectual friends.
"You can find me in my garden",
I tell my green thumb pals.
"You can find me in my forest hideout",
I tell my environmental cronies.
"I'll be out on the lake",
I tell my fishing buddies.
But if you want to find me,
I'll be right here on these pages.
You have turned to this page
Because you want to know me.
And now you do.
In the end
I want to be with you.
Because you understand me.
Alone with you
On these pages with you.

"The distinction between past, present, and future is only a stubbornly persistent illusion."
~ Albert Einstein

IN THE UNIVERSE

THE CIRCLE OF INFINITY

Infinity disappears into itself
And becomes a circle in time.
It spans its own creation,
The circle of the universe,
Wrapping itself into itself
Recreating itself unto itself.
Becoming creation anew.

Existing in itself in this
Ring of continuity,
Infinity encircles the energy
We emit as mortal beings,
Mirroring the circulation system
Of the life it creates,
Escaping our mortal limitations,
The sundial, the clock, the wheel,
To mimic the unbroken circle of our lives.

The path of infinity moves
Unconcealed in a band,
The only perfection,
The unboundless ring.
Around the circumference of
Ours and others' planets.
We attempt to stop and
Sketch a circle in the sand.
Only to have it disappear
When washed away by time.

INCONSISTENCIES

The snowflake and the autumn leaf
Can cause you charming disbelief
When you settle them in your mind
Alongside descriptions of humankind.
Metaphysicians have been thinking
As the universe embarks on shrinking,
That they can deftly explain
When walking backwards on a train
That related celestial radioactivity
Describes a theory of ancient relativity.
But in the leaf is a simple map
That science will never unwrap
Confirmed by a snowflake in its glory.
A shrinking universe? Not to worry.

VIBRATIONS

There's a rhythm in nature
That's in tune with your heartbeat.
This music of the body
Flows like a brook through one's life,
Swelling at times
In spirited flood,
Subsiding in times of quiet content.

At age sixteen,
All sentient mortals
Have the chance to connect with this rhythm
To flow in its grace
And share with others its nuance.
This rhythmic vibration among mortals
Permeates the harmony of the universe.

You can sense it in the sound of the surf
And the vortex of a summer storm.
It undulates in the aurora borealis
Or the eddy of a typhoon,
In the humming of the locust
Or the thrum of the jungle.

Do you hold dear
The gift - this cadence of vibrations?
Or have you, like many, remained deaf, insensate,
Crippled by the roar of industry
Indifferent to the connections?
If you are not yet sixteen, consider this.

THE STRAIGHT LINE

Ah! The straight line!
Pure in its beauty
Clean and effortlessly
It slides forward
Into eternity.
Coming from infinity
It continues on
To pursue the connection
With itself.

And when it does connect
The snowcaps will melt
And deserts will crystallize,
Oxygen will singe the clouds,
And forests will char.
All mortals will cease
To serve up progress,
And fellow animals
Will have finished their charge.

The straight line
Is where we have been
And where we effortlessly go,
Avoiding the dissident, the diversion,
The defector to our destiny.
I cannot go back.
Give me the straight line.

CATCHING TIME

No one has figured it out, yet.
The sun will come up, no need to fret.
The moon rises, no sweat, no threat,
On all this, --you can bet.

Time, -- it's the hands on my clock,
It's a stifling cellblock,
Crucial seconds in a wok,
The aftermath of wedlock.

"So why all this concern, honey?"
"Well, losing time, --it's never funny."
"Yes, time marches on, Sonny."
Can time really sabotage money?

If on your wrist you wear a watch,
A saved minute is not a botch.
And you can always gain a notch
In life's marathon and such.

Daylight savings time opens a door,
I gain one hour from the day before.
If I die and fall to the floor
I will have lived one hour more.

Try killing time and you will find,
It puts you in a constant bind.
You'll forever be behind.
Oh, heck, never mind.

I haven't figured time out yet.
And as in Rome: tempus fugit
To wretched time I am in debt.
I'll take for now, what I can get.

THE ETERNAL CYCLE

Shards of flesh are the substance
Of all activity on this planet,
And I suppose, on other planets, too.
Fueled by unchosen vapors
(Like oxygen and nitrogen).
Some evolve to a boney structure,
Others choose a slimy skin, thank you.
Some (who are shy in nature)
Select a crusty shell or heavy armor.
Some feign weakness.
(Others are truly feeble.)
Some arise to be valiant,
Others just appear that way.
A few burrow, others fly.
One thing is constant:
They all eat each other,
Alive or decomposed.

ME, MYSELF, AND I

Fruit fly, do you ever see yourself
As some part of a great scheme
Where you are just one part of a system
That is so large and expansive
That even humans can't tell you a quantity
Even if divided by one quadrillion?

Fruit fly, can you see yourself
As a member of something greater
Than your complex whole
That must abide by dogmas
And mythology that resides
In ancient scrolls and pages?

Fruit fly, can the history of you
Date back to rumblings of beginnings
Where I chose the correct path
And you hesitated and became
Something less than great with wings
That could fly about as me?

RAISED TO THE POWER OF TWO

We have been absorbed into the skies
On this moonlit evening
By the precise draw of the planets.
Propelled by the force
Of chosen love
We stay gloriously traveling
Where the power of gravity
Compliments our boundless thrust
Of energy and love.

The knowledge of existence
Draws me closer to you
And we become partners,
Held in inverse suspension
Leaving behind those detained
By the inquisition of others.
We are raised to the power of two
In this celestial voyage,
In a new realm where
No others have realized
This interlude of bliss.

ORDER

Einstein gave us a formula for gravity

And, matter, and of course, that good ol' energy.

His manner of speaking was rather terse,

Describing the '1930's universe.

He preferred everything to be in order,

Up to the Milky Way's far-off border.

But there's something strange, and missing coherence.

It's the way he dressed in public appearance.

When you'd see his familiar head and face,

You'd expect to see every hair in place.

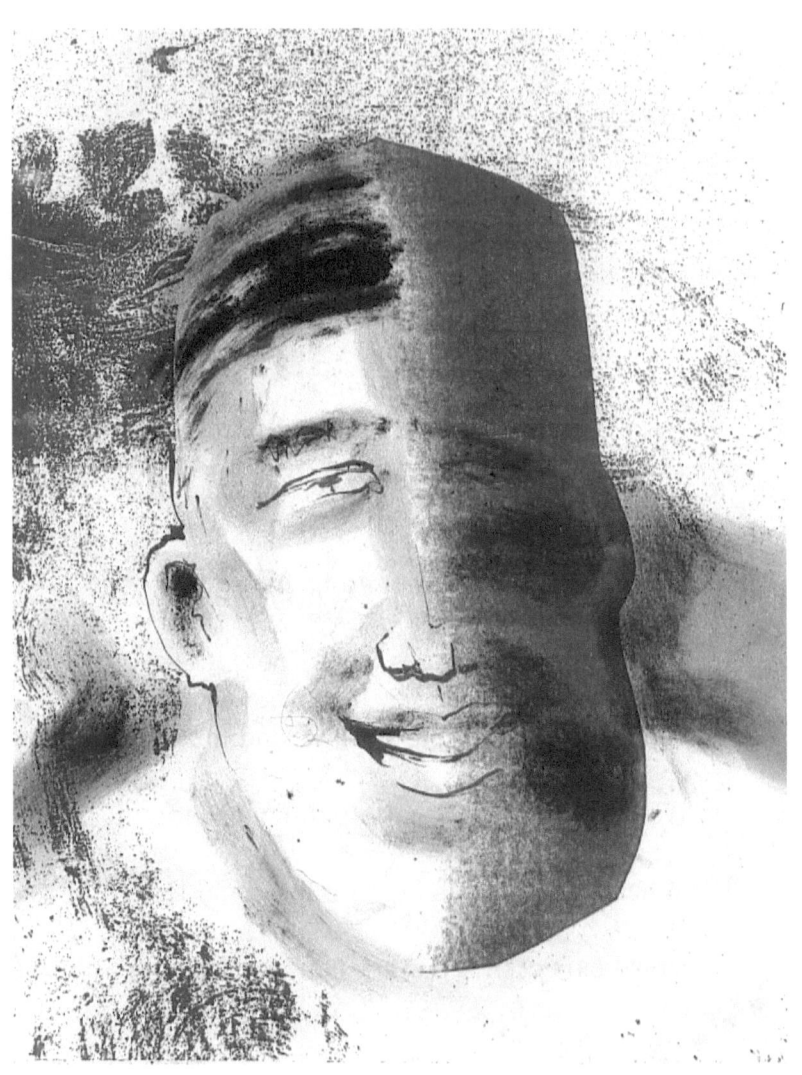

SPRINGING FREE

When was it?
When have we done this before?
You've come into my life, again.
From somewhere.
I renew this love once more.
It is fiery, and vast...
An exploding sky entity.

I am weak with wonder
That you are here again.
The planets lock into infinite pattern
For a nanosecond
And we spring free,
To float motionless
Quietly, together, forever,
Into eternity.

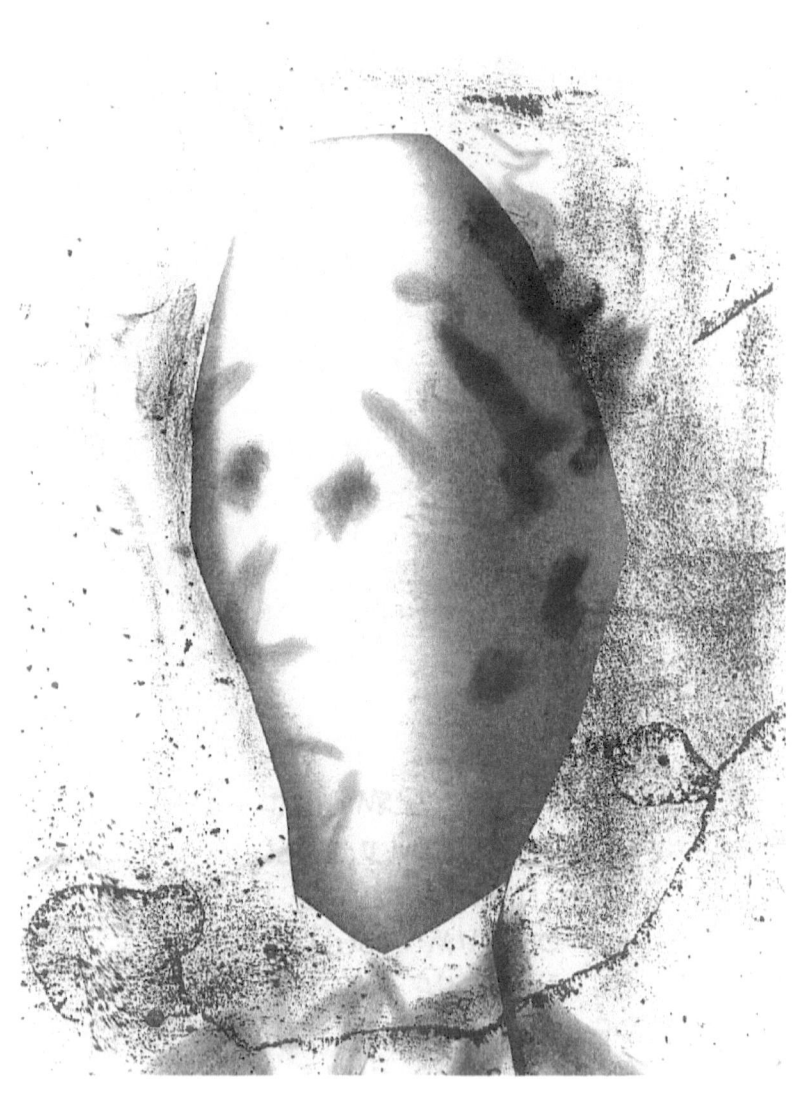

CELESTIAL CHEMISTRY

When troubled sleep comes upon me
And relentless cosmic currents
Arouse my restless skeleton,
A wave of euphoria spreads
From my hairline to my liver threads,
And I quiver with rapture.

Far beyond my imperfect eyesight,
I cruise out like a comet
To the suburbs of our universe,
To asteroids and other objets du ciel,
Where protozoa can be the size of Jupiter
And bacteria are big pearly balloons.

I visit the center of Uranus and Mars,
Examine the energy of fission,
The immutable logarithms of chemistry,
And speed to the black side of the moon
Where I sleep until dawn.

ELECTROMAGNETICITY

There is no measurement
To the distance
That separates us, when you are gone.
Even though the moment be brief
It is as if
The electromagneticity of the cosmos
Has sucked you back through space
To redistribute you among past eons.
Now when I cling to you
It is with fear -- with apprehension
That perhaps mere chance
Has blessed us with these precious moments
That might not survive
Until dawn.

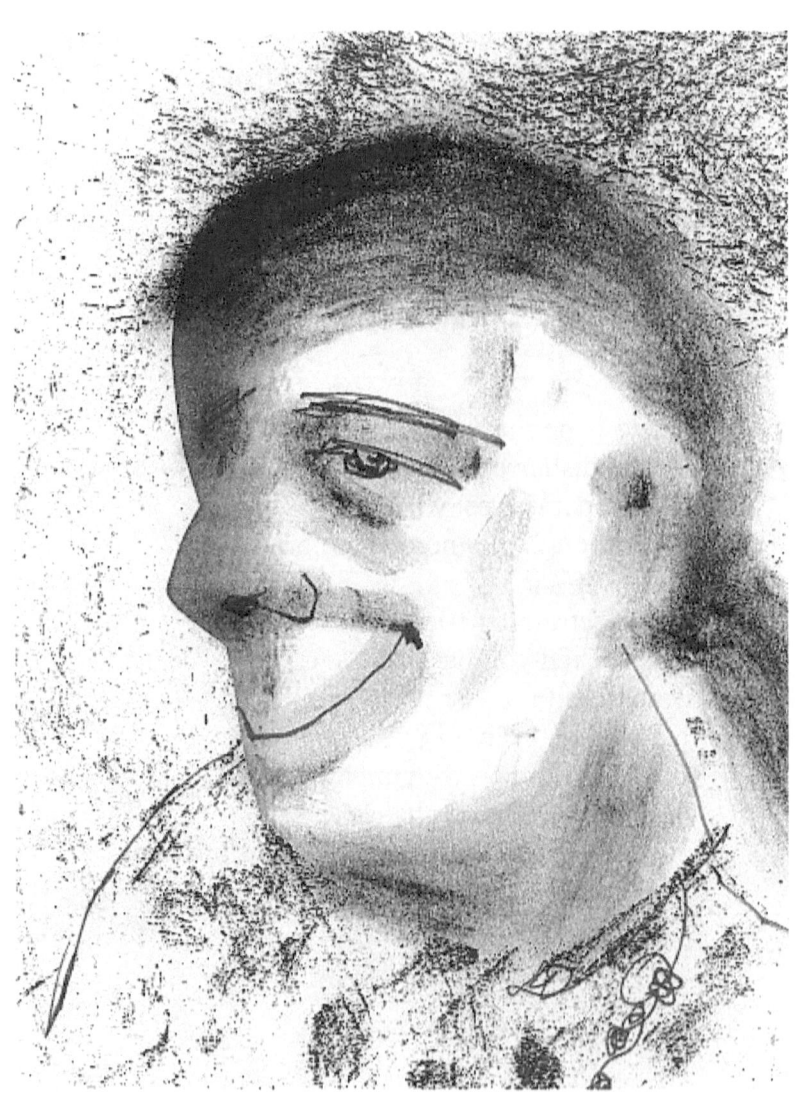

FAREWELL TO MEASUREMENTS

Along the beach
We uncalculated ourselves
From the measurements of life.
We unbolted the inches and grams
And loosened the centimeters
Of our foolery.
We pressed hours into nanoseconds,
And poured years into cubic feet.
We gathered these computations
And with an abacus of pebbles
Counted all digits of disgrace,
Mixed them with a quart of love
And in a millimeter palm leaf boat
By starlight,
Sent it all off
To a gallon of world.

I PAINTED A SEASHELL BLUE

Eventually they'll all be blue,
Light blue, cerulean, azure, violet blue,
sapphire, primary blue, turquoise, cobalt,
teal, navy blue, Mediterranean blue,
bright blue, dark blue, blue-blue.

It's only by accident they are not blue.
The sky is blue, the sea is blue.
An accident of DNA has made them
The color they are.
But I will change all that.
I will make this one blue.

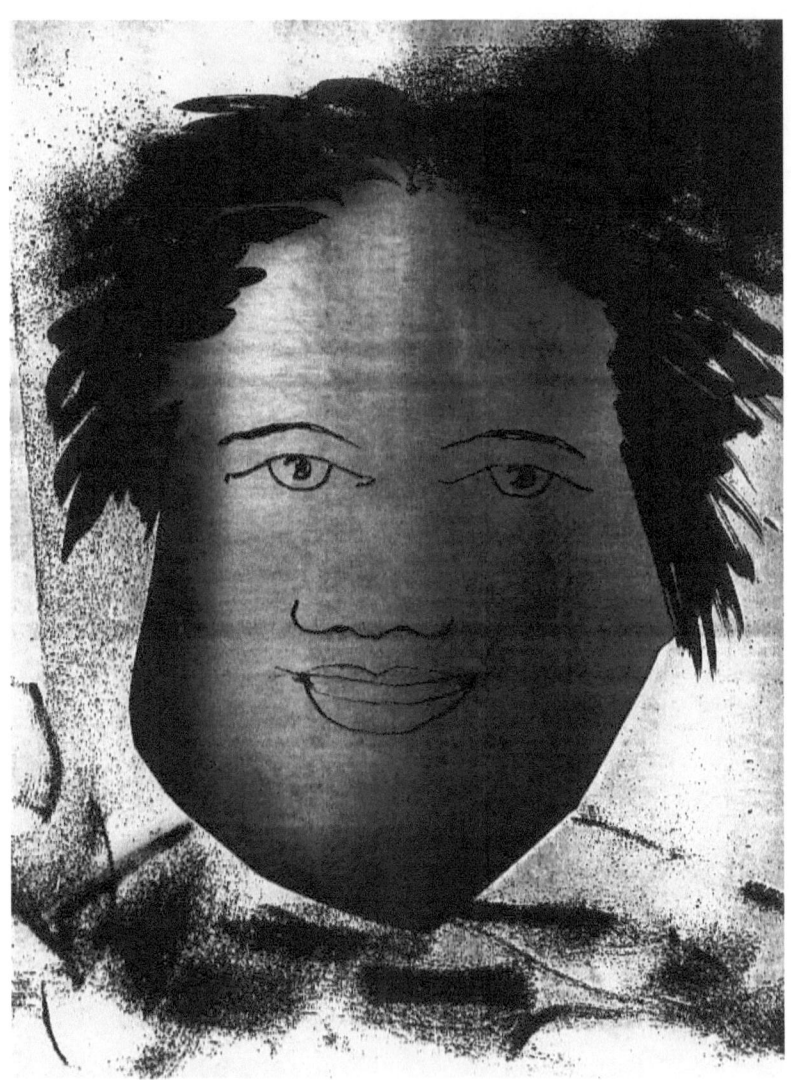

ZERO

In those days
We had the time
To understand the beauty of numbers --
To decipher digits and their
Numerical values and quantities --
Of related domes and spheres.

We would sit and count the wind,
And multiply it by leaves,
Then add to it some relative rain
Plus a quantity of sea.
And divide all this
By nothing...or something.

In those days, we understood this:
The greatest mathematician
Knows nothing of zero.

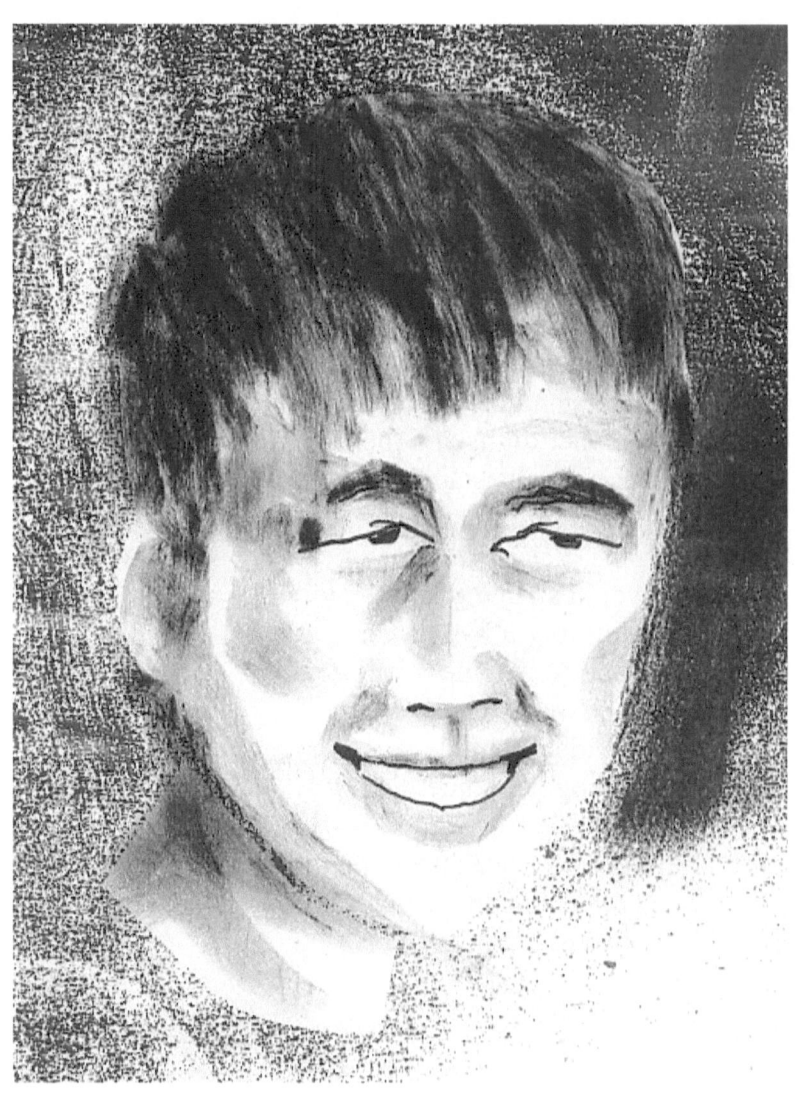

MINE TODAY

One certain day, mayhap in a billion years,
We each will come to own the earth
For one day.
Your day may come after you are gone,
Or before you are born,
But the mathematics and electronics of living
Might cause the Roulette Wheel of Circumstances
To Land on Today,
And make the match of supreme chance.
Yes, one day it will come to you,
If you have not known it before,
And you will say to the world,
"The earth, it's mine today!"

THE MAGNET WITHIN

What is this magnet that I find
Has control of this wanderer's mind?
With my aging and my learning
Has come a stirring, constant yearning.

A memory flow I cannot shut
Builds up filings in my gut.
They form a magnet in my soul
I am hopeless to control.

I am to my homeland drawn
Where my nascent seed was spawned
Where my mental lava spills
The outcome of my raw ideals.

Others may resort to cower
In a life gone painfully sour
Still others hold to safe retreat
To find security complete.

But I instead choose bold deliverance
To searing, captured boyhood remembrance
For making a life that will matter,
There's no doubt: I choose the latter.

Where my life with joy unfolded,
Where my soul was tenderly molded.
Whether it spins out wrong or fair,
Or ends in righteous full despair,

Do we have where e'r we roam,
An unseen tug that tows us home?
This magnet is in our lovely soul
That guides us to our final goal.

"There is no cure for birth and death save
to enjoy the interval."
~ George Santayana

THE JOURNEY

DISCOVERY

Ah! Felice . . .
You looked the other way
And then you found it.
Was it when you were thirteen
Or twenty-three?
The mystery disappeared.
The gate was open
And spring flowed in
And you rushed out into summer.

You discovered you -
With smile serene
And alluring hands
And solid breasts
And impenetrable loins.
Who would know
Your secret of passion,
Your treasury of desires?

And now in the winter of life
About to arrive
To wrap you in solitude,
You are no, not alone.
While others look back
At tombstones of memories,
You continue your lively gait
Head high and glinting eyes
Feeding off your appetite
In your passion of enchantment.

VOYAGE

With no direction I plan my epic voy
  age. No time destination beckons me.
I move amongst the heavy earth clouds
Where lurk the beasts of happenstance.

At dawn I head in the direction
  of our star
And allow a millennium of
  millenniums
For my arrival somewhere on
  this planet
After countless seasons have passed.

From the crags of stone mountains
And the slippery slate of cliffs,
Below in the summer moonlit midnight
I view the crevices of lush valleys.

Onward seeking the vegetation of life,
Ponderous creatures move in
  dull rhythm,
Their young follow in cadence,
Their elders decide the direction.

Above, enormous birds circle in quest.
Their skinned wings stretched
Like drum skin saucers
They descend effortlessly as umbrellas.

I soar with them to the waters
  below.
My splash goes unnoticed.
I emerge beside a laden log
Refreshed and energy full.
My journey continues on
Through thick lagoons of
  vegetation,
I paddle through murky waters
Sending ripples messages to the
  shore.

Through the millennium …I
  have traveled,
Breathlessly admiring the
  landscape
Of rushing streams and deep lakes,
Ever seeking refuge.

Now ashore again, I stand erect.
A tribute to my endurance,
A prize unto myself.
Refreshed and alive, I journey on.

I AM OBLIGED

Since the day that I was christened, I've been obliged to closely listen;
Required to surrender my attention, to follow the rigid stream of convention.

Bird and man and insect all, we move on swiftly lest we fall.
Through dark of night and misty morn, in swirling wind and heartless storm.

Blindly I follow the surging flow, knowing not where it will go.
This is my destiny, I cannot pretend, knowing not where it will end.

I look about and try to find some other obligation for my mind.
I wrestle and struggle until I'm spent, in this sorry and futile attempt.

The far off hidden sea nymph speaks, an ancient upstairs floorboard creaks.
I cannot remember a single day, a murmur has not turned my head its way.

But who's to say I've not done wrong, being passive and going along
With this parade I find myself in, is the outcome better than where I've been?

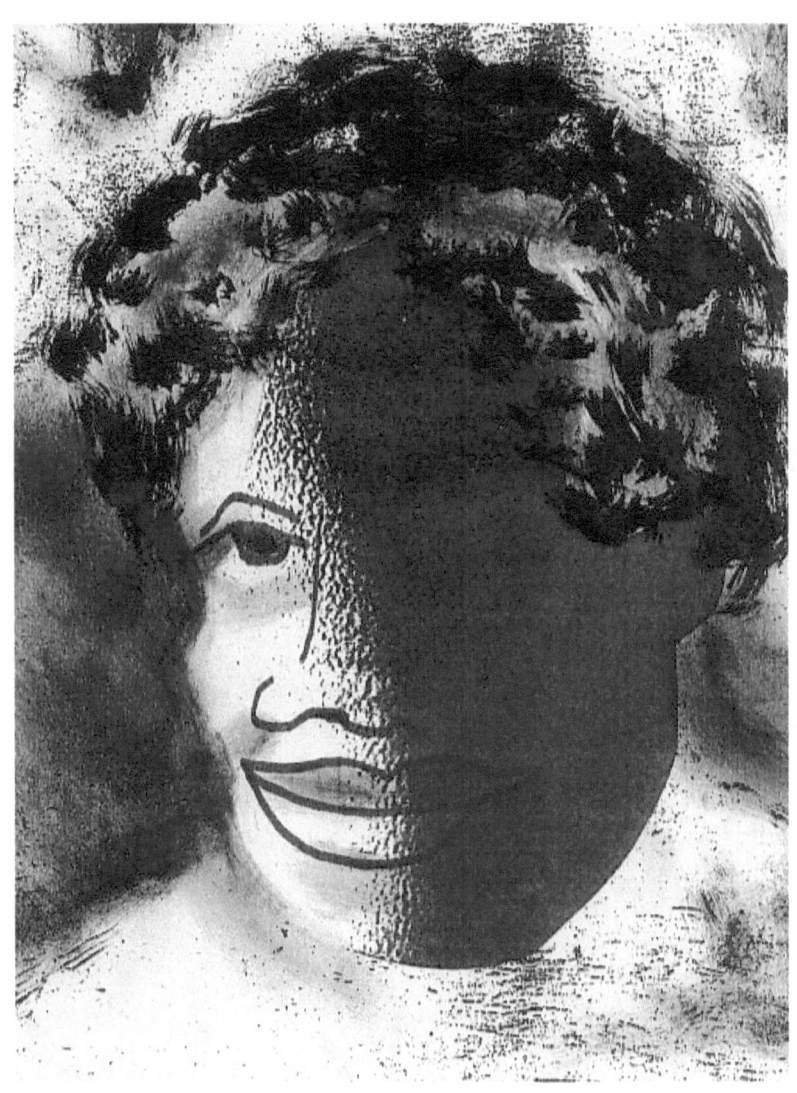

ODE TO A CAVE ARTIST

When others were gone hunting and gathering,
You, the invalid, the fragile one,
Were left behind to tend to the young and the fire.
In a crevice of your mind you invented.
Vibrant images tumbled and struggled
To burst free from your imagination,
That others might see your worldview.

With simple dye and lumps of carbon and ochre
You placed your visions onto rock walls.
But your eloquence was short-lived.
Constricting conventions of cave living eclipsed your mission.
Your superiors, with the need to control, forced you
To sketch to their demands
For the rewards of food, warmth, and protection, you yielded.

Lest you be pilloried a heretic,
You followed their dictates, born of their suspicion and fear
Of your unusual talent. You portrayed only animals,
Never Man nor Woman, lest you suffer the penalty.
But one day, on walls deep in a clandestine cave,
Your desires found life and you began depicting
The forbidden motif, Man and Woman,
In this silent dark cathedral illumined only by torch.
You glorified the unthinkable: Man and Woman,
You secretly returned many times to your hidden gallery
And gave birth to many paintings.
We are still searching for them.

THE PATH

I have seen the path through the woods,
One that has been journeyed
By deer and fox and then
By dog and man.
And I say, "I wonder
If this would be better,
To start over there."
(Where there is no path).

It's my nature
To start over there,
To struggle through brush
And vault over fallen logs,
Ignoring the sting of sharp rocks,
The burn of thorns and brambles,
Never considering going back,
Not knowing where this
Path will lead,
And eventually to experience
What no deer, fox, dog or man
Has yet discovered.

NOTRE DAME

Only the scavenged tombs
Of the ancient civilization survive.
Stretching out beneath its towers,
Vestiges of a well-planned city
Once known as "Paris"
Along a tropical river,
The Seine.

Covered by lush greenery
These many centuries
Since the ice broke free
And the waters rose.
Notre Dame, said the faint inscription.
A 12th century cathedral
Struggled within the
Steaming jungles of Europa.

Like an Egyptian tomb
Once glorious, domineering,
The cathedral remains there,
Hoping for less silence,
Maybe the sound
Of a welcome footstep,
Any language will do.

Only subsistence natives
Exist in Europa,
Once thought to be the seat of
A flourishing civilization
With thriving trade and commerce
By land and sea.

But it will be
Another 150 years
Before a young archaeologist
From Antarctica University
Discovers this lost culture
That once flourished
Beneath the greenery
Of this tropical land.

NEW START

As a boy, I would dream aloud,
In comfort with the breeze.
I'd ride up on a soft white cloud
Or skip among the trees.

I loved the smell of
  rain-washed grass,
The bird song in the rush.
The innocence of a lovely lass
Would make my body blush.

I grew into a youth mature,
Bronzed with hair of blonde.
I loved a lass, lithe and demure,
We vowed to keep our bond.

We blossomed first externally,
Then fought with worldly dues.
Increasing hurt internally,
We clashed with painful views.

We tried and tried to follow course
To find ourselves a balance;
We strove in vain for wisdom's force,
And shattered our alliance.

Now I'm of that grievous lot
Whose countenance shows the
  story.
My mind and body have
  been bought
By lucre and corporeal glory.
.
I am no longer that innocent boy
Whose world lay pure before
  him.
My limbs no longer radiate joy
Of life with bliss and whim.

I have become the other side
Of what I should have been.
My indulgent ravages have not
  lied.
It's time to begin again.

ETERNITY

When you were then,
And then was before,
And before was fine,
And fine was perfect.

Those were times, we
All believed we were
The best of buddies
And cool, and strong.

Then the avenues of
Change, and highways
Of transformation,
Took us for a ride.

When you were then,
And then was before,
And before was fine,
And fine was perfect…

Now we are here,
And here is now,
And now is forever,
From this time on.

-

278 K.Y.A.
I am awoken by the stench of the
  hairy wolf
Sniffing at my hut. He and his
Agitated teenage pack scratch
  excitedly at the
Barricaded entrance to my hovel.
I add more kindling to the fire
And thwart their bold attempt.
They whine at their failure.
They move on. My family returns
  to sleep.

178 K.Y.A.
We have not known clear sunlight.
The frost of July will not leave us.
The lush vegetation of our
  grandfathers is gone.
Our nut kernels have become   rancid.
The landscape has fallen into
  shades of gray.
The bone-thin gazelle is our meal.
We have become the meal of the
  stealthy tiger.
My shivering family sleeps in darkness.

1078 B.C.
The mighty Magyar has come
  and departed,
Leaving charred ruins of our proud hut.
Remaining are three of seven children.
Wifeless, I look for another mate.
Horseless, I dig the soil for another crop.
Only the mighty and strong live in caves.
Homeless, we sleep high in the shelter
  of trees.

078 A.D.
The Emperor's forces have enslved my son.
A Roman mercenary has stolen
  my daughter.
My home has been claimed by foreigners.
I join the trail of weary emigrants,
And along the road find a new mate.
We settle in a protected valley
And raise a proud family of three boys,
Who learn the language of the
  conqueror,
And sleep in the garment of the battle-ready.

1078
An emissary has brought word
That our King has proclaimed war.
My sons and I will be called to battle
To defend our homeland and our
  King's crops.
We will wear the noble colors of our faith.
We wait for orders from our leader.
To prove our loyalty and allegiance
We fight willingly against tyranny,
To protect our possessions
And the peaceful sleep of our daughters.

2078
From the screen on the wall
Comes the message from the supreme
  command.
Today's advice and current rules
For pure thinking and a clean environment,
And instructions for self-protection
Against the evils of inner-terrestrial invaders
Who might steal the frightened minds
Of our sleeping wives and daughters.

AT 30

His life had just begun
At twenty-one

He didn't know what to do.
At twenty-two

He exited society
At twenty-three

A roving troubadour
At twenty-four

He was in overdrive
At twenty-five

Still the maverick
At twenty-six

Still breathing oxygen
At twenty-seven

Began to pollinate
At twenty-eight

Found his valentine
At twenty-nine

And

Lost his liberty
At thirty.

MY SEVERAL SELVES

In my place on this planet I've often tried
To alter my senses, let the muse be my guide.

I let my imagination stray on to myself,
Letting my mind wander into itself.

I trek on this journey entirely alone,
To a destination completely unknown.

Today I'm slave, tomorrow referee,
And the day after that, who shall I be?

The route is lined with friends and mourners,
Predictors who'd lead me into dark corners.

Now and then I rest 'neath a tree
To contemplate my destiny.

I recount the delights and seeds that I've sown.
And play back all the memories I've grown.

Bound to this path, I'm firmly resistant
To those who'd ask me to be consistent.

For myself, I believe, the dilemma's my own,
There's no one to help me, I find I'm alone.

There are several selves in me.
Yet few of them do I know or see.

This uncertainty is destined to worsen.
It's alarming to know I'm no single person.

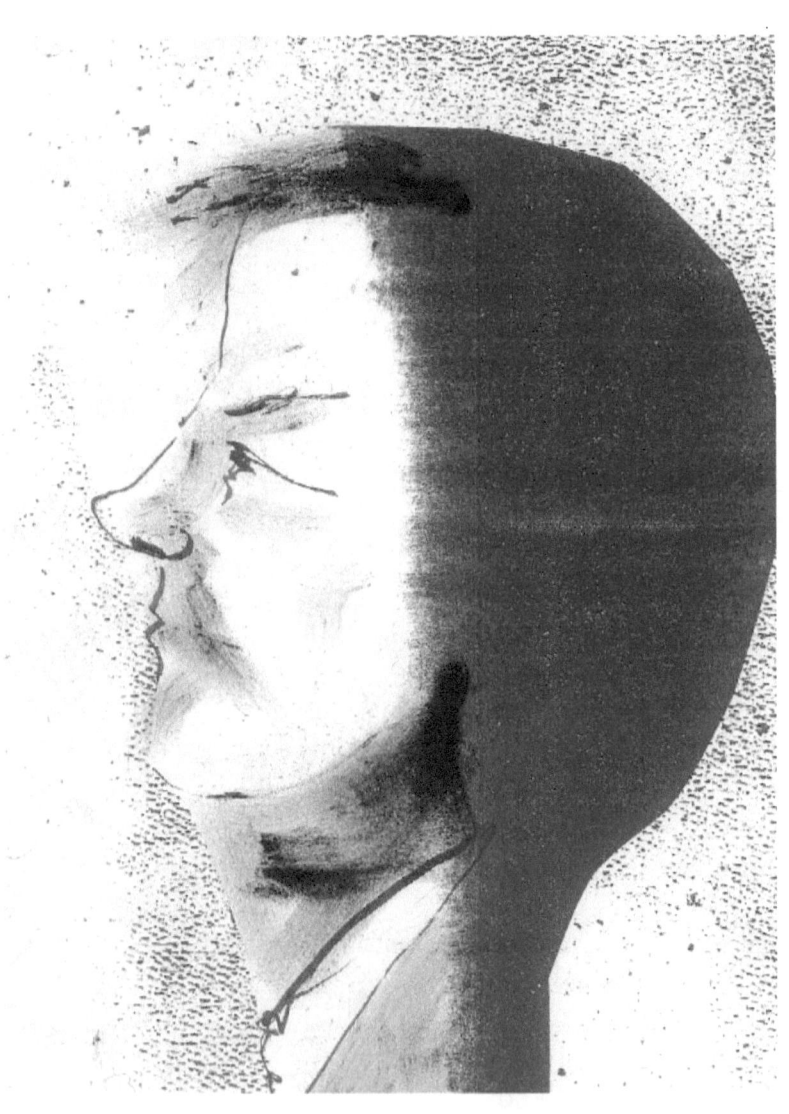

ANSWERS

When I was young,
and being an unruly brat,
My sentences usually started with,
"I can answer that."

And now that I'm mature
and wearing a different hat,
I answer like a worthy adult:
"I do not know the answer to that."

EARLY MAN BECOMING

I am Early Man.
I have evolved to become
A body structure of accumulated sinew, flesh, bones, tendons,
Ligaments, muscle, thew, fiber. The framework is in place.
I can hear long distance when I place my head to the ground.

My eyes can spot a procompsagnathus or saltoposuchus a mile away.
My brain is large enough, now. I will find flint to make a spear
Sharper than the tusk of a boar.
Eventually I will invent a longbow and a crossbow
And other weapons.

I kill, eat, excrete, copulate; kill, eat, excrete, copulate.
For millennia, I do the same.
Kill, eat, excrete, copulate; kill, eat, excrete, copulate.
I can do better than this.

I will make a trap by the waterhole and ensnare the unwary beast.
I will make a fire in my shelter that will give warmth forever and ever.
I will gather the eggs of the turtle, and capture the fish with my seine.
I will plant seeds and discover the seasons and store the reserve.
I will invent language and song. I will invent stories and music.
And weapons.

I will learn remorse and how to revere and bury my family dead.
I will find pleasure in beauty and solace in pagan thoughts.
I will invent an afterworld to give meaning to my existence.
I will discover friendship, attraction, and cooperation.
I will become enlightened and profit by wisdom. I will dream.
I will assemble knowledge and I will dream and dream.
I will profit by leisure and dance and painting and learn writing.
I will be careful, and care for my offspring and my mate.

I will listen to stories of my Ancients, those who once lived in trees.
Eventually, I will become as swift as the antilocaprid
And fly as high as the olden archaeopteryx and be strong as
    the tyrannosaurus.
I will have the armor of the allosaurus and be as clever as the rurestris.
I will ride on my eophippus and train it to plow my territory.
I will visit the moon and migrate to the heavenly bodies of nighttime.

No longer will I fear the roar of the anilocaprid, or archaeopteryx,
I will become hominid and I will develop new weapons.
And rule all evolved things on this planet and in the night sky.

VIGILANCE

At my cabin window pane frosted with winter white
Except for the heated circle where a blood-eyed wolf stares
Watching my fireside warmth. He is intent on finding sustenance
For his frigid family afar. Sometimes he sees me as entertainment
Sometimes as food.

I make contact with this Ancient wolf, in repose at my fireplace bench.
We both share the inner space of this central meeting place,
This equilibrium. This Ancient and me.

This reenactment of ancient times is without fanfare - or applause.
We know that we each have predators to us both,
And have no guarantee that can quiet our fears.

Bright embers utter instructions that direct us to a flicker
Of flame that will bring a kindling message of vigilance
That entwines the snap of sound and the warmth of useful destruction.

We sleep, this Ancient and me, and sleep for a million years.
When we awake the blanket of remnant embers
Has faded to ashes and joined the darkness of our past.
We are compelled to move closer to engender warmth,
Completing the cosmic cycle that has not changed.

Again, at the window pane, the no-name wolf stares
Intent on finding sustenance for his frigid family afar.

The withered fire has faded from neglect,
And we each in our own way go into the darkness
This Ancient and me to fetch the fuel and overcome the fright
That is embedded in our genes.

A CHANGE IN WIND

The sails of my journey
Have learned to adjust
To the whims of news headlines,
Ambulance calls and fire sirens.
I can now absorb the detours
And sense the disasters.

Oh! If I had known
The treachery of my sails
In the early days of this pilgrimage
To the land of symmetry,
Where reaction takes on action,
Where negative marries positive,
Where zero adds to plus minus plus.
I would have foreseen the battles lost
And the wars won
With soul still intact
In the change of wind.

MOMENTUM AND FLOW

Like zebras of varying stripes
Stampeding to unknown destinations
We are led by unseen forces
Enchanting us to follow.

Protesters following a voice,
Pack wolves following a scent,
Brown leaves following a brook
Ants following their winding trail.

We go, sometimes casually
Sometimes in blind awkwardness
Sometimes purposefully and knowingly
Few of us remain in complaint...

We sacrifice our minds
To the massmind of the momentum,
And we accept the movement
And move with the masses.

Here they come, you will join them,
Swept up in the vortex of excitement
And the fear of banishment
The fear of namelessness.

Those who are brave to resist
Are left to start a new movement
Gathering new adherents
New victims, new directions.

*"The violets in the mountains have
broken the rocks."*
~ Tennessee Williams

THE KINGDOM
OF NATURE

RABBIT IN THE SNOW

Through my cozy window pane
Our eyes meet.
Always with your startled look,
You pillory your intrepid gaze upon me.
Should I wish my world upon you?
I am fat and unhappy.
You are lean and frigid.
And intrepid.
We compare our differences.
Shall we trade?
You, for my 72 degrees of comfort?
Me, with your freezing fright?
I think not.
I'll die slovenly and warm.
You will be found this spring
Frozen stiff in a melting snow bank,
Unable to express your lost chance.

BIRDS AND INSECTS

Birds are nice
But insects are beautiful.
I have made a request
To the GrandMaker
That in the Grand-Remaking
He, or she
Will reverse the order.
That is, birds will become tiny
And insects will be the size
Of starlings and crows.

Since there seems to be
More insects than birds
On the planet
And since insects bite people
More than birds do, anyway,
There would have to be some laws
Against insects taking over the world.

THE SECRET OF THE GRACKLES

It's November and it's election time. And it's the time when grackles
Congregate in our farmyard trees, as many as 50 dozen at a time
In preparation to migrate south.

They are loud. Oh, so loud! It sounds like a political convention.
Like snow geese, they need a leader. But unlike geese, when they make their
departure, they don't fly off in orderly manner.

But their actions are much like politiciansand supporters of politicians.
They cannot agree which direction to fly. A couple dozen fly off to the east
But they return, disappointed with their leader.

Another dozen, especially loud ones, fly off to the west,
Expecting others to follow.
They again return to our farmyard tree, disappointed with their leader.

Another bold group flies straight up to the sun, but returns quickly
As if they were on a test flight. If I wait long enough, they all leave together.
In the meantime they are voting on resolutions, deciding on destinations.

What or who makes the decisions for them? Did our screen door slam,
Or the catwalk by, Or did a cloud pass over the sun, or a gust of wind
Sway the branches, or did one boisterous grackle dominate them?

In the middle of my sentence they just flew off all together as a group
Looking like a spray of gravel in the wind, rising, winding,
Dropping, sputtering, cackling like crows, arguing like hornets.

I watch them fly across the north 40, heading curiously to the north!
A splinter group breaks off, maybe five or six and flutters, bends,
And heads off south. A straggler joins them.

By the time this tiny group has flown over the lake, the large group
Has veered sharply to the east, now headed south back towards me again.
They pass over, cackling, veering, rising in unison.

A slimly white blob falls and splats on me...As they head south.

THE SCALE OF IT ALL

The tiny entrepreneurial spider,
Squats silently, contemplating
He spins his empire-to-be,
In the idle corner
Of a public outside staircase
Where giants ascend and
And society rumbles
The little fellow toils away,
Unaware of the magnitude
Of his dream of achievement.

He surveys his domain.
Should he conserve his strength?
Take a nap? Hope for inspired arousal?
Or disallow the nay-saying environment
And actively expand his empire?
Leaving his fate to wind, rain,
Big shoes and other known vultures?
Or just grow fat, gobbling up
Other unfortunate arachnids -
Large and small.

Or will he spend his days
Procreating and contemplating
What could've been.

NOVEMBER MORNING

At the top of the hill the nomadic school bus
Blinks its warning light, stops and looks
And then lumbers on with its bundled cargo.
The mailman's car appears around the bend
And pauses at the distant neighbor's mailbox.

I turn the picture calendar page
From October to November.
The postcard pumpkins of October
Give way to frolicking finches in the snow.
And out my postcard window pane
The frost-carved trimming shows
Ice fingers edging the tree top twigs
As a field mouse scampers across
The chiseled snow path to the barn.

A nuthatch in the feeder
Steals another seed from the mother cardinal.
From high in the naked crab apple tree
A squirrel nibbles a frozen remainder morsel
And then spews pits to the earth below.

The plump once-white snow is
Like a freckled girl turned 40,
Heavy, and tired already,
Mixed with November sticks and leaves,
As gray as the sky,
Becomes rigid and the temperature drops.

NIGHT FLOWERS

Exquisite flowers that frolic in the night,
Are flowers undiscovered by sight.
Instead, they yield their pretty clothes
To flowers that you can find - - with your nose.

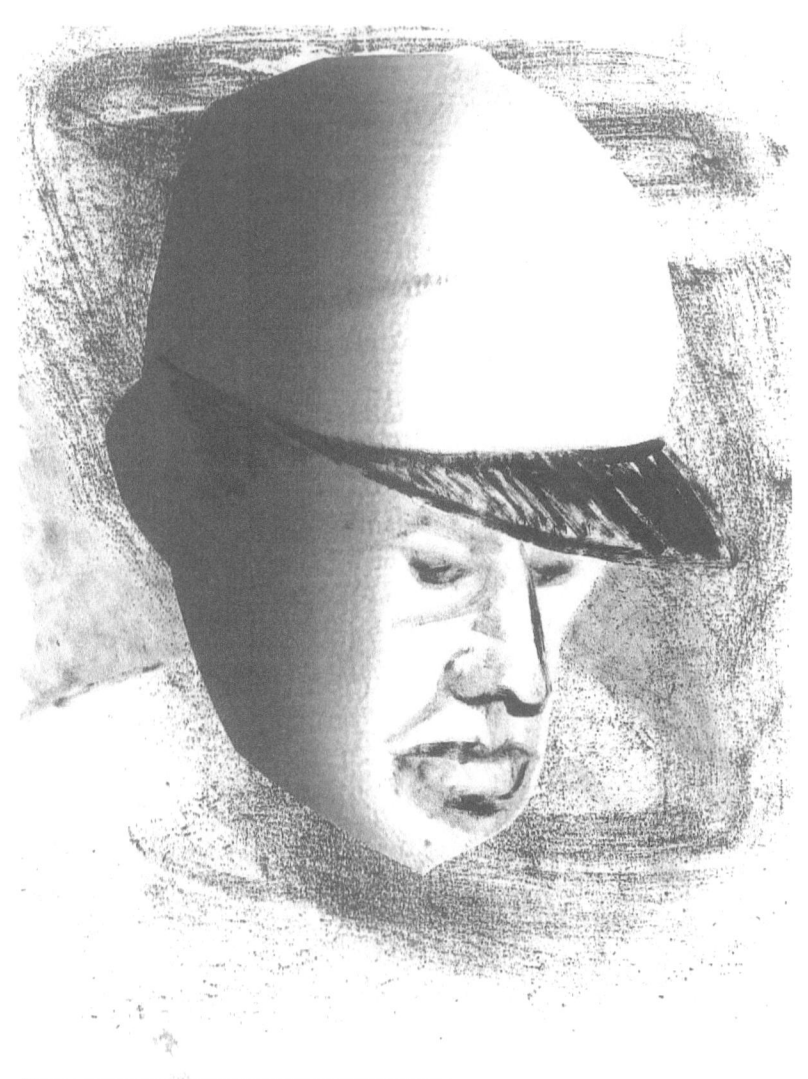

I'M THE STRONGEST DOG
IN POLK COUNTY

He scratched my head
As he has so many times
In the past.
And it felt good
Even though
I'd rather he would've
Scratched my back.
And now it is the future
And I lay here with no appetite
And no desire to drink water
And no desire at all
Other than to have
Him scratch me all day long.
I'm weak now
And can't walk
So I lay here
Having dreams about
When I used to walk and run.
He would tell me
I was the strongest dog
In Polk County.
But today, he was not convincing

To me or to himself.
I heard him on the phone
Calling the Vet
Saying he was going to
"Put me down."
He mentioned Friday.
If "I didn't go before then."
Now as I lay here
With only the tingly feeling
Of shock in my body,
I imagine that he is scratching my
  head
And saying that
"I'm the strongest dog
In Polk County."
And I'll hear him say that
All the way up to Friday.

INSECTS

Beyond imagination are
These fellow creatures of the planet.
Intriguing in their design
With marvelous engineering,
Gossamer wings
Rugged war-ready legs,
Eyes that have the power
Of a television tower.
And stingers that can kill you dead.

Insects allure you with their beauty
Like Communists to their plan
Or Terrorists to their commitment
Or Fascists to their rewards.
But I must not let them fool me.
For when the day is done
They must be eliminated,
If nothing else because
These insects might bite
My young daughter, Mary.

HOW ALIKE WE ARE

On my way to the mailbox this morning,
I should've worn mittens and a scarf.
It's only a 100-yard walk, but a bit frosty.
The 20 below zero weather was not bad,
But the wind sent the chill down to 50 below.
My ears felt thorny and my nose like a popsicle.
The snow on the road crunched under my boots,
As I approached our lonesome mailbox.

Suddenly he walked out of the woods
And stood on the patchwork of snow and macadam,
A six-point buck, pompous and healthy.
Big tar-colored eyes and slick shorthair hide,
He stood his ground and tapped his foot in announcement.
Was this a handshake or a challenge?
I took it to mean he wanted to share something with me.

As our eyes met they said "Hello fellow, do you think as I do?
"Are you wondering what will become of us?
"Will we make it through the winter?
"i have no answers. but we are alike."

DEERFLY

A storm is brewing
And the deer flies are buzzing
Around me as if to ask questions.

Upon consideration
I'm going to run for cover
For them I have no suggestions.

FROZEN TOWELS

Drifting snow at my winter watch.
The farm is one big ice cube, all 100 acres.
The January window pane will crack
If the temperature drops another degree
Or the wind shifts from east to north.
Arctic living in Wisconsin invites derision.
"I told you folks not to move up there!"
I see the those towels left on the clothes line,
Frozen like Napoleon's banners in Prussia.
Those towels will be left there 'til April.
Who will trudge through 25 inches?
Reminders from someone's October check list,
Dangling from clothes pins in their winter bliss.
Frozen towels like Calder's swinging mobiles,
Sentries waiting for the thaw of the coming Spring.
"What else is left undone?" you ask.

CATCH IT IF YOU CAN

The black winter night
Hovers over me
With meaningless intention.
This veil of mystery
Enshrouds my steps
From house to barn.

A sparkle of light peeks and sinks
Like a shameless window display,
Catching my attention
And then disappears
Behind a nightcloud swiftly.
"Catch me if you can."

I stop to breathe in the aroma
Of frozen branches
And fallen twigs
As unsleeping birds calculate my footbeats
In the crunching snow
On my now forgotten mission.

I am too youthful to know
That these moments should be scrapbooked
And filed cerebrally without emotion.
For they are a dash of proof
That I am here;
That I am eligible too.

WHEN APRIL LIGHT

From this wretched trench
Where gutter folly survives
Within this bigot shell,
Where an irksome mind
Leads a chorus
Of discarded chants,
I will start anew
And emerge restored.

April light and Spring sounds
Will unearth a life in me
That will survive
This hollow winter of misdeeds,
Of broken self-promises.

My valiant purge
Will expel the invaders
With piercing objectivity.
Musty winter thoughts will depart,
To cleanse my blood
To wash my pores
And scrape my hide.

Awakened by the April light
My life will emerge anew,
My soul scrubbed clean
With the April light of Spring.

TREASURE

Over my shoulder
I could sense they were there,
Each fruit slightly swaying
In the late evening breeze.

In this dark hour they vanished
Into the moonless blackness.
But there were still days left
Of this year's plump crop.

In the folding summer evenings
The fruit often summoned me,
Glistening and auburn
On the stalwart, alluring tree.

On my jog the next day
In the mellow radiance
Of the fruit-filled hillside
The tree beckoned me again.

But, alas! No time.
I would charge on
Believing there was
Still, another day.

SNOW HOSTAGES

A slight wind from the east.
The snow began falling officially
In the afternoon on November 30th 1971.
At chore time, I put on my Mackinaw and mittens.
My 10-year old, Robby, and I began shoveling
A path to the woodpile, and one to the barn.
Lights from the kitchen window outlined our progress.
Out on the nearby county road,
I heard the sound of a car chugging forward through the snowdrifts.
Its red taillights disappeared into the brewing blizzard.
As I shoveled my way back from the barn,
Bending into the blustering knee-high snow,
A wisp of white smoke curled sideways from our chimney.
Robby had already gone back in
And started the fireplace kindling.
Blowing snow blew back the kitchen door as I entered.
A cheery fireplace blaze,
And the aroma of cinnamon and cocoa greeted me.
My wife, Sherry, draped my soggy mittens on the fireplace screen.
We gathered for the evening radio report
That announced there would be no school tomorrow.
And punctuated by gleeful whoops from our three children,
We all munched on warm cookies.
The snow continued throughout the night.
About 3:00 a.m., a whistling sound like several fifes
Rapping outside my bedroom window woke me up.
The snow was now blowing sideways.
Sherry and I checked on the sleeping children.
In the morning, I rekindled the fire.
The snow had piled up against both doors. We were sheltered in.
The radio reported that snowplows could not get out to do their work.
Sherry prepared Swedish pancakes.
The children continued to sleep like soldiers on rehabilitation leave,
Not knowing this 32 inches would be the record snowfall of their lives.

CONSISTENCY

Rolling over pebble after pebble
The river flows predictably,
And progressively spills
Into eternity, taking with it
Helpless soil, and autumn debris,
In consort with the ashen moon.

The river lies in wait for winter,
To gulp fallen snowflakes
And turn them into frozen crystals
Of pure fractal movement,
Until the thaw of April,
When, impulsive and recharged,
It flows onward into gentle summer.

With consistent touch
Like Anthony Dvorjak
Or Ted Williams
The river surges forward
Following an irreversible theme.
Like a postulate, a sure bet,
A foregone prophesy,
Toward its target.

It's an unstoppable equation.
It molds us into style
And shows us what to imitate.

THE ETERNAL CYCLE

Shards of flesh are the substance
Of all activity on this planet,
And I suppose, on other planets, too.
Fueled by unchosen vapors
(Like oxygen and nitrogen).
Some evolve to a boney structure,
Others choose a slimy skin, thank you.
Some (who are shy in nature)
Select a crusty shell or heavy armor.
Some feign weakness.
(Others are truly feeble.)
Some arise to be valiant,
Others just appear that way.
A few burrow, others fly.
One thing is constant:
They all eat each other,
Alive or decomposed.

"My religion is very simple.
My religion is kindness."
~ Dalai Lama

BODY AND SOUL

SATISFACTION

As reasonable humans, we all strive for joy,
And a state of being, sort of like heaven.

Now I've been thinking, when I was a boy,
I reached that condition once, back at age 7.

WHEN WILL I MEET MY GOD ?

I've been told there is a God.
But lately I've been told there is no God.
Now if there is no God
It does not matter when I meet God
Because I will never meet God.

But if I ever meet God
I will say, "Lord God
There are a lot of people who say, "God
Does not exist, so don't depend on God."

I wish I had a way of relaying this to God.
You'd think I'd hear from God, by now.
I wonder if there is a God.

CRAWLING HOME

I submit this statement:

I harbored my abundance of delights
And placed them in a secret cache:
A protected refuge: My lovely camouflaged
Shell.

I have divided myself all these years,
Allowing reflections of realness
Never to pierce this impenetrable
Shell.

I have severed more than half of my beliefs
And yielded to the elements of greed
And wallowed in the delights of my outer
Shell.

I have detached what goodness was in me
For reward of the elements of appetite,
Only to retreat into this weakened
Shell.

Yea, now the throngs of dark militia
Advance as vermin over my body,
And I retreat to the trenches to what's left of my
Shell.

End of statement.

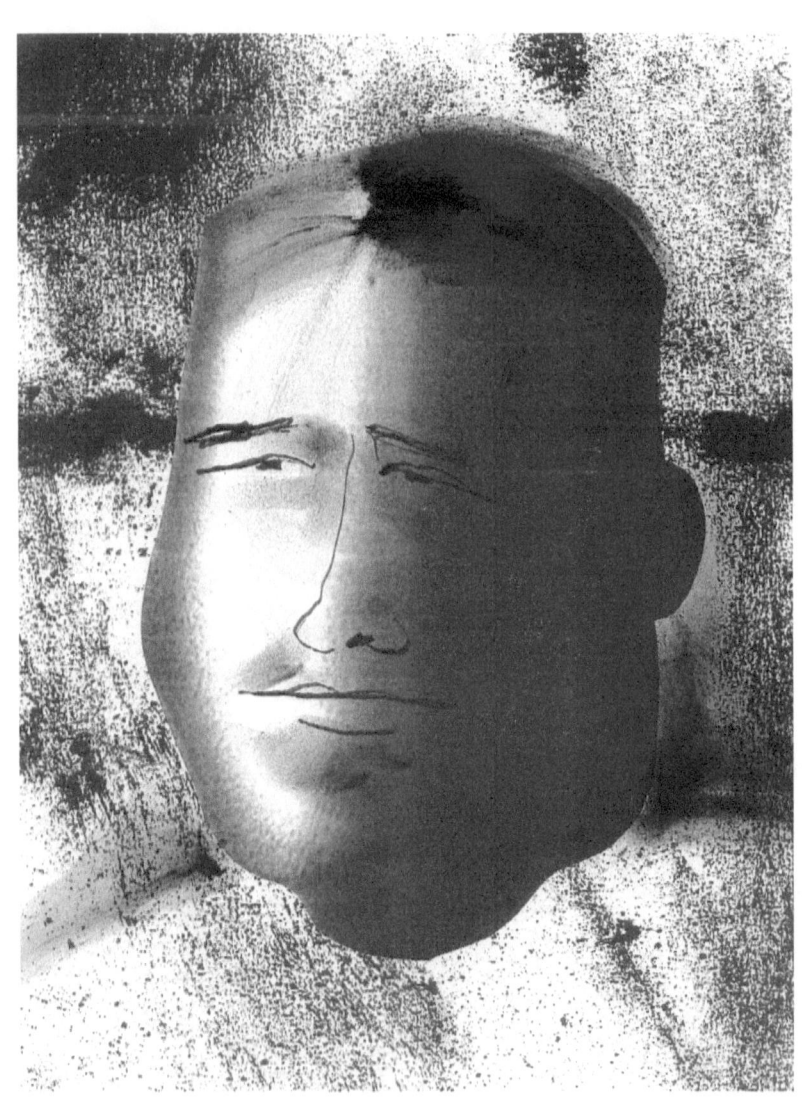

UNSTAIN MY SOUL

When Spring light and April sounds
Unearth what life survived.
I promise myself
There'll be a new man born
Within this bigot shell
Where gutter nonsense thrives
Like sewer yeas and sludge.
Where demons emerge
From wretched trenches
To stain my soul
With flakes of weathering prose
From coats of pristine pride
And gargoyles lead the chorus
Of hollow chants and jeers.

But Life is suddenly anew!
And musty thoughts are not reviewed
Awakened by the April light
With frightened objectivity
New thoughts emerge
To refresh my soul
And cleanse my liquors
To wash my pores
And scrape my hide.

Once again I am alive
Spring light and April sounds
Will unearth what life survived

I'M LEFT HERE ALL ALONE

Quietude permeates this room.

It is a tangible scent of doom
Not the haze of opium nor ether
For I'm a taker of neither,
Not the sweetness of burnt matches
Nor the linger of smoldering ashes.
The after effect of a final song
Or an explanation all gone wrong
No description can say it well
This preview of eternal hell.

WE NEED A NEW SPIRITUAL LEADER

The time has come to look around
A trusted leader must be found.
Not the kind with crumbling truths
Whose evil deeds corrupt our youth.
Nor do we want someone callous
  and sinister
(Who indeed might be your parish
  minister)
Nor someone bored and world-weary,
They've gone and fled to a monastery.
And beware the man who would
  be leader
Whose only attribute is the theater;
Or someone in their run for power
Who seeks unfortunate souls gone sour
When they've got them in their clutch.
They offer them a shallow crutch

We need a person of moral mysticism
Who is not righteous to our criticism.
Beware the slogan: "God's on
  my side."
If each one says it, someone has lied.
We don't need religion that's more
  of the same,
We no longer want to play that game!
Religious wars have taken their toll,
Fist-shaking and torture to win
  your soul.

The lobbyists for God will get
  you scared
"You'll land in hell! so be prepared!"
Or, "Don't step out of your
  local crowd,"
They dictate that it's not allowed.
"The world is ending!" they
  will say,
"Fall to your knees and begin to pray,
"Lest you suffer the penalty
"Damned to hell for eternity."

Let us emerge from this skullduggery,
And turn away from all this drudgery.
Our path to freedom has been aborted
By leaders who've managed to
  distort it.
People allowed to speak their mind
Choose spiritual freedom of a
  different kind.
God is not happy with what he's seen.
He's ready now to wipe
  the slate clean.

CROSSING OVER

Today's agenda is full
My calendar is bloated.
Some say I am a fool
That I have turn-coated.

I know I am sober
And have not lied
I am crossing over
To the other side.

INTERRUPTION

My little brothers and sister knelt at the edge of my mother's bed as we always did during lent at 4:00pm when we came home from school. The family rosary was in my mother's hands and she pressed the beads as we said our Hail Marys. I was the oldest at 13 and we were praying for my father who was working at a temporary job in a war defense factory up in Wilmington, Delaware.

There we were, all five of us, kneeling around mother's high bed, and my neighborhood friend, Gilbert, baseball glove in hand, knocks on the door and walks right in shouting, "Elmer, can you come out and pitch some baseball?" And since my mother's bedroom was just off the parlor, and the door was swung wide open, he looked at us all as if we were newly arrived aliens.

My mother kept the Hail Marys going and stared at him and then me sternly, nodding her head to signal that I should usher him out. But I couldn't. After seeing the gawk he gave us, I kept my head down and chose not to look at him. Before I muttered anything in return, I heard the screen door slam. That was Gilbert's last visit to our house.

FOREVER IN SEARCH
OF SOMETHING STIMULATING

I emerged from the womb a natural born man.
When I go to my tomb I will be as I am.

I will seek out pleasures: foods and hard spirits,
I will take wild measures and never fear it.

I will smother sex and heights of sensation,
I will become a lover of extreme temptation.

Nothing will hold me, no synagogue, or church.
Nothing will impede me in my persistent search.

I'll clutch jubilation through dishonesty and stealth.
If I don't find stimulation, I'll devise it myself.

I'll die all forsaken, with exploits known well,
No angel mistaken, I'll end up in hell.

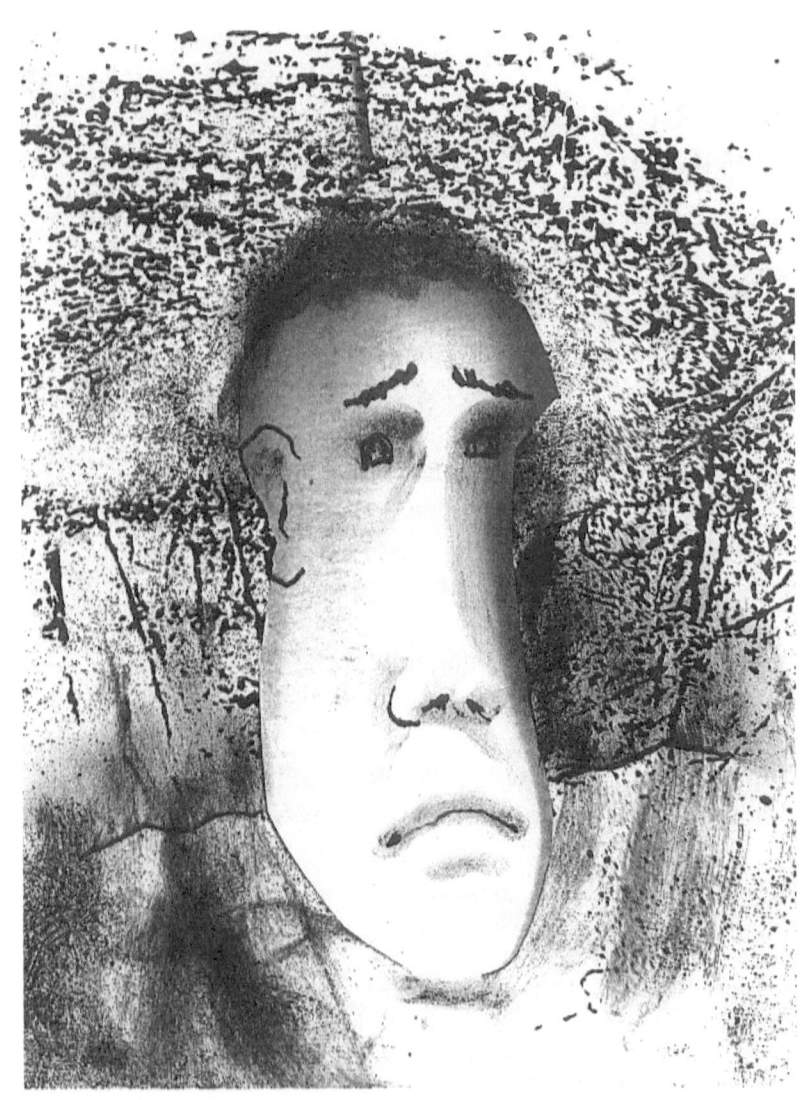

Not every medieval scribe was literate in the language...
maybe because Noah Webster wasn't born yet.

Whylom there was a squier who coude nought wryte nor read.
So this povre wight seyde these words to me:

BENEDICTE

The shrewe wind blows
Into the cracks of my povre hovel
And morewe commeth the schnee.
Nathelees I have noon mede
To have nought dout nor pleyne
Than to met of flour and feere
Because wostow I am worthy

Pryvely ich dorste to deme
That my arwe of coy love
Is entente on you.
Your gyse and goost
Gives me ese,
Ich breste with love
And everich ywis kan
That I am trewe
And worthy that you
Wod trowel to be my trewe love.

Forthye, ich dorste to axe
For alderbest,
That you may have fey
Canstow foryeve my woodnesse
To wene that you would rathe seye
Ich do .
Benedicte!

COMING SOON

Will it come to pass?
The word is out again,
You'd better go to mass.
And review the Commandants Ten.

To me the thing that's troublin'
And hard to figure out,
And got the folks a bubblin'
Why there's so much doubt.

If you're prayin' every day
And hear the tollin' bell,
You're going to heaven anyway
And that is sure as hell.

NO PROFIT IN DISTRESS

I come this long and woeful trail
To seek not fortune nor Holy Grail
But quiet nook and peaceful grace,
A contemplative gentle place,
To rest from storm with safe protection
And dream of His inspired direction.

My pursuit is true and filled with bliss,
Free from evil and heavenly kissed.
The encounters I witness along the way
Serve as crypts where we kneel to pray
To rid ourselves of ignorance
And find at last deliverance.

In a world of conflagration
We watch the destruction of our nation
Where treacherous men cause toils and woes
That feed on spoils of others' souls.
We'll rid ourselves of wrongful knaves
And choose a path to rightful ways.

We cannot depend on the winds of fate
To favor our dreams, no matter how great,
Life is learned in one great lesson:
Stalwart decisions give no concession.
It's from the heart that we stay pure
If we as a nation plan to endure.

As I rest here in sheltered repose
My thoughts go on to those who chose
To engage their lives in doleful fight
To protect a canon they felt was right.
And burned at the stake or die by the noose
For efforts to rid our land of abuse.

I can hear the mournful singer;
I have the choice to stay and linger
Or move forward and forget this pain
Like others before who have done the same.
My anguish will vanish with success.
For I know
There is no profit in distress.

PRAYER

God, if you do exist
You should not be interested in me.
I do not pay you allegiance
Nor offer you a morsel of my mortal flesh.

Here I am, though, talking to you again.
You have tired of my rantings
And try to ignore me, I know.
And I commend, your fine success at that.

And as for all the others
Who are much more important than me,
I wish them good rewards
For their whispered announcements to you
Clothed in selfish verbiage.

You, God, are not someone or something
That I would want as a friend.
For you have done too much harm,
If indeed, you do exist
Somewhere.

UNAWARE

Late winter
In times like these
When misery takes possession
And unnamable spirits
Settle heavy upon us,
No reasoning opens avenues of escape
No answers surface.
We sacrifice ourselves
To the mercy of circumstance.
Young and ignorant of our condition
We battle each other and ourselves
Groping, twisting, flailing
Separated as if by winter blizzard
Or flash floods of the coming Spring
Unaware that this time will pass
And reunion will come.

DEVIL-GOD

If the Devil does exist
Then he be you and me.
If the God does exist
Then he be you and me.
If we exist
Then we are the God
We are the Devil
We are the God-Devil
We are the Devil-God.
Today I am the God
Today you are the Devil.
Today you are the God
Today I am the Devil.
And tomorrow?

I CAN HEAR

What I hear
Is more than others hear
And I know it's true
Because I shiver when
A sound comes to me
And I swell and
Internally stammer
To myself
When these sounds
Enter my body.

The world is
Twice the world
For me,
And I am living
A second life
Others Hope for
In their prayers.
And all because
I hear so well.

"A problem is a chance for you to do your best."
~ Duke Ellington

BODY AND MIND

MY SEVERAL SELVES

In my place on this planet I've often tried
To alter my senses, let the muse be my guide.

I let my imagination stray on to myself,
Letting my mind wander into itself.

I trek on this journey entirely alone,
To a destination completely unknown.

Today I'm slave, tomorrow referee,
And the day after that, who shall I be?

The route is lined with friends and mourners,
Predictors who'd lead me into dark corners.

Now and then I rest 'neath a tree
To contemplate my destiny.

I recount the delights and seeds that I've sown.
And play back all the memories I've grown.

Bound to this path, I'm firmly resistant
To those who'd ask me to be consistent.

For myself, I believe, the dilemma's my own,
There's no one to help me, I find I'm alone.

There are several selves in me.
Yet few of them do I know or see.

This uncertainty is destined to worsen.
It's alarming to know I'm no single person.

CALENDAR

Oh Calendar there upon the wall!
Tell me, you've been around awhile,
Who's the greatest fool of all?

The months flip by like a movie screen.
I'm up, I'm down, I'm in between.
So many hours and days unseen.

Clicks o'clock and the desktop chime.
This thing you sell, you call it time.
Some of it wasted, some of it prime.

You've engaged the sun, the moon,
Morning, evening and afternoon,
Calendar names like May and June.

I need a calendar to measure
Appointed days of peace and leisure?
Why should squares dictate our pleasure?

You're the fool, for pity's sake,
I'll take a break and eat my cake.
Oh Calendar you're the big mistake!

REVELATION

"Know thyself," the philosopher said.
"Shouldn't I already know myself?" I asked.
"When you're six feet under and dead," He said.
"The world will take off your mask."
"And what will they find?"
"Nothing they didn't know before."
"Then, the world's impression of me
Will not have changed after I'm gone?"
"No"
"Then why should I 'know myself'
If it leads to changing myself,
I'd rather be who I think I am
Than who others know I am."

THE GLANCE

You have, or will have:
The experience
The mystery of
"The Knowing Glance."

No, it is not
"Do I know you from somewhere?"
Nor, "You look just like…"
Or, "I'd like to wake up in the morning with you."

You'll know when you receive
The Knowing Glance.
Awareness of it hides in our genes.
Its power is woven into our instincts.

It is a riveting recognition.
A flicker of profound perception
By someone who sees into you
With respect, or maybe, anxiety.

It bespeaks an unspoken language
As ancient as cave paintings
Or pictographs
From our primordial forbearers.

The Knowing Glance
Discovers your soul
It touches your essence
You will feel its discovery forever.

SWELL

So here we are
This you, you, and that other you.
And we look, look
Without struggle
To see, see, see.
And what we see is
What we think, think, think.
("Try to stop thinking.")

My grip on your wrist tightens
It is not like the truffles
That you ordered for me.
It's something new, new, new.
("Just try them.")

I defy you to re-invent
What we had.
Korea and Chicago re-visited.
And The Beatles
And some other group
We both can't remember,
Remember, remember.
("Just try to forget.")

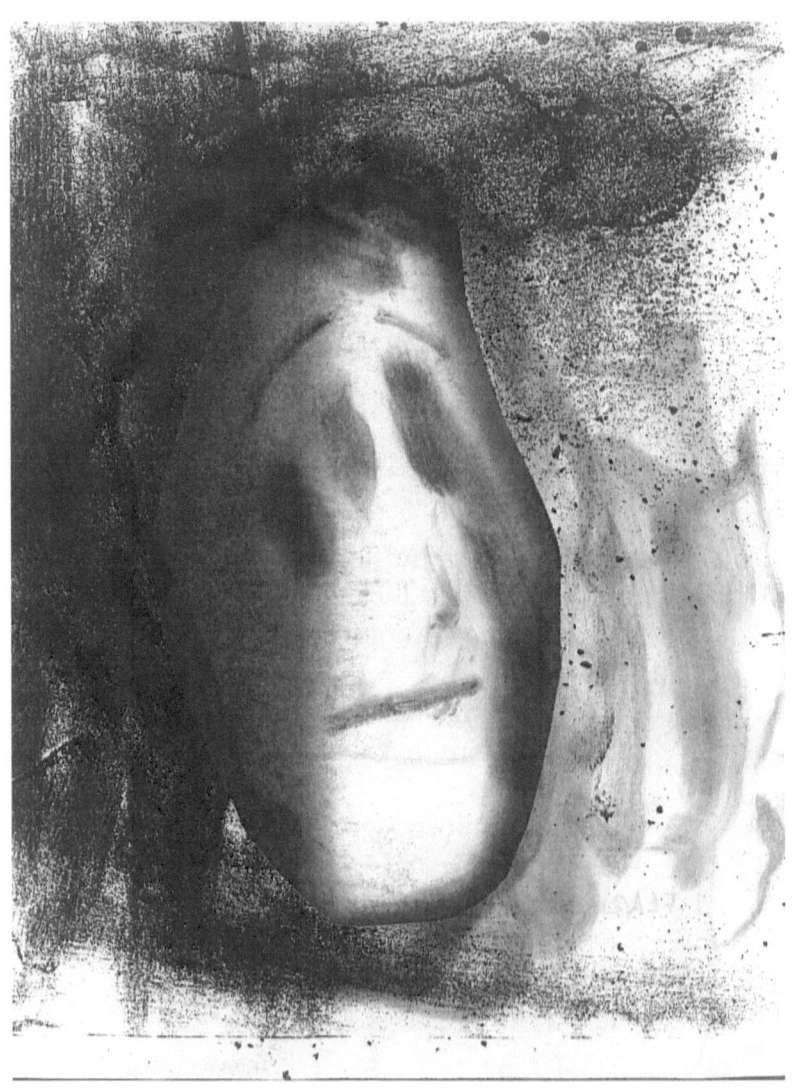

ANTICIPATION

In my brain there is a stimulant
That represses boredom and ennui.
It dwells as a refreshment
To the thirst of my longing.

Unlike other planet creatures
Who are unaware of their future
Who exist to prevent destruction
And live in fear of extinction,

I have this special place
Where I can crawl as embryo
And see the future of my happiness
In anticipation of excitement.

I thrill to the thought
Of its coming, of its arrival,
As the moon wanes in shadow,
As the sun rises in its arc.

It's out there lingering
In a quiet upper room
To be seen and felt
By me alone.

NIJINSKY

He leaped into the sky
And alighted on a thin line
A gossamer thin membrane
And held on to look down on us.
He listened to us
From his air on high
Hearing what none of us heard.

They declared him insane
Because he saw us
And listened to us
From heights
We could never attain.

They put him in a white room
With one window
With thick walls
That would not allow sound to enter.
But, still, he heard.
And there he stayed for 30 years
Very able to listen
To what we can never understand.

DARKNESS

It moves like smoke
Wrapping itself with strangling intentions
Around my movements, present and perceived.
It suffocates my senses with fear and suspicion
Heavy with odors of threats and bad performance.

This is the darkness of day
That dances a clown of sadness in my path
And chills my temperament to cold blue.
Dark creatures gliding above identify my flesh
And dreadful beings wing toward me.

Yes, this is the darkness of day
But soon, real darkness, the soot of night
Will descend onto my earthly dwell
To comfort me with silence and sightlessness
And I'll be alone in the cozy black of my room.

WITHOUT DIMENSION

My life has been without dimension.
My writing has gained me no attention.

Some consider me just a fool,
A receptacle for their ridicule.

How can I cease the jeer and sneer?
What if I were to cut off my ear?

SUNSET GRAY

This swamp is soggier than those I knew
As a child in our backyard bayou
This eternal sunset gray
Accompanies me as I stray
Far beyond those limitations
Into even murkier premonitions.
Of dismal blue or charcoal hue

My feet sink deeper with every step
And here I creep where others crept.
Emeralds dissolve to jade along the way
The greens fade into sunset gray.
The sounds of animals I never knew
The smell and stench of charcoal blue.
I descend and sink, and call a name.
The sound returns, I hear the same.

What are your thoughts on this soggy swamp
Where indigo fog paints a macabre hue?
Do you come here as I do?
Do you speak the tongue of the jasmine root,
Or play your dirge on the quagmire flute?
Do you hear the words of the soggy swamp
Where moss of emerald green is seen
During the days of sunset gray?

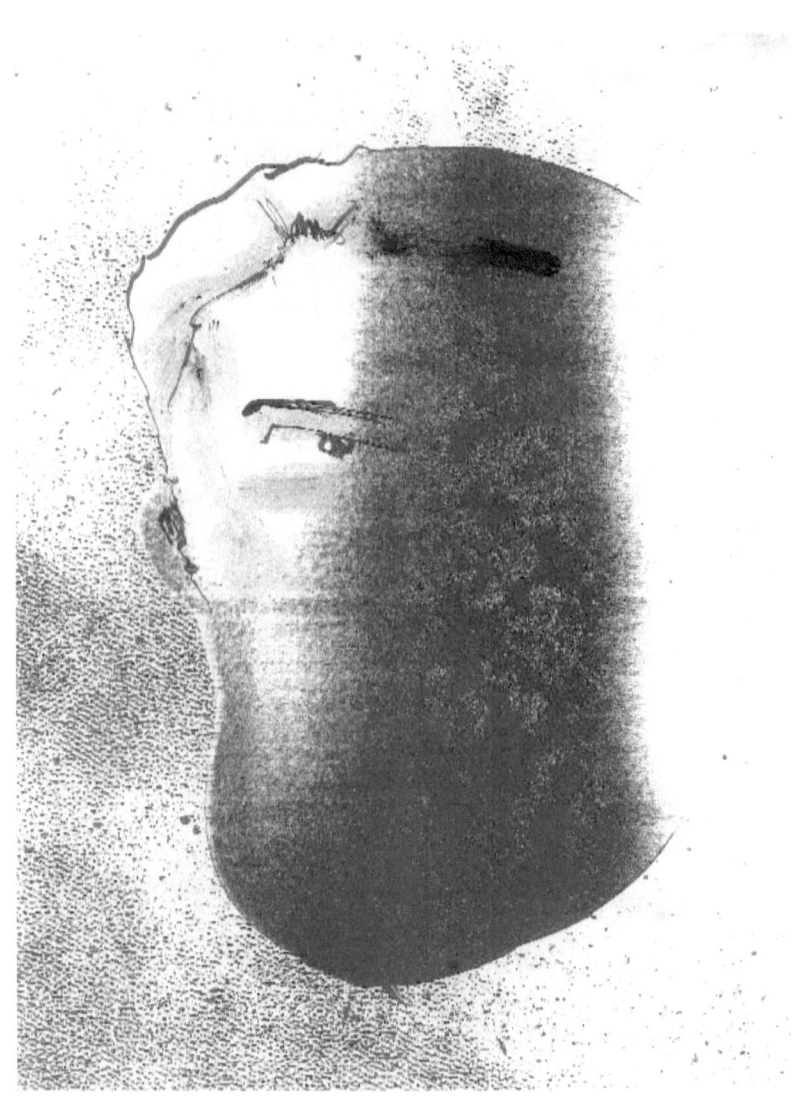

MY LIFE

This must be the point in my life where I will be
able to look back and say I gave up on my dreams.

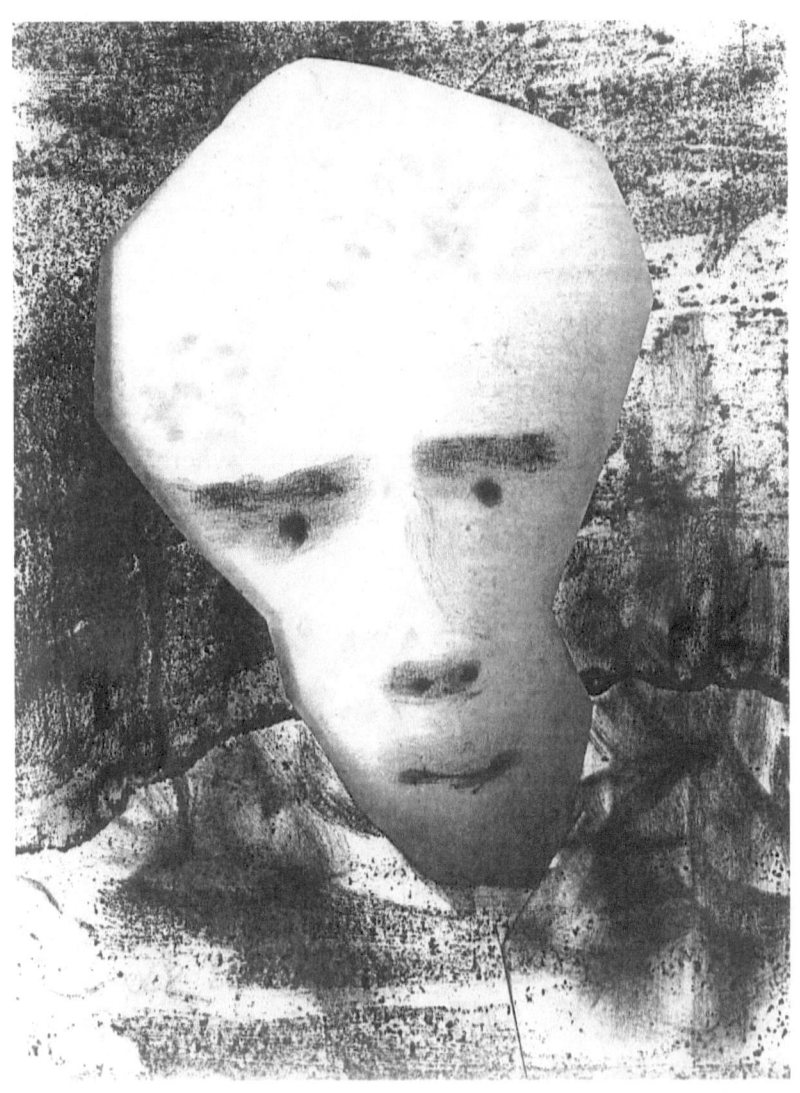

EXHAUSTION

My synapses refuse to connect,
A spray of ether engulfs my body.
My lungs gulp a shallow wisp of stale air.
My weary legs hang from my hips.
My joints squeak. My ears ring. My hair hurts.
I try my voice. It's a noise from my throat.

From my brain I hear commands to recoil
And I flinch, but in slow motion.
I am too tired to sleep, too weary to think.
My heart is drumming at a slow drag,
My blood moves with no rhythm.
I am being, but nothing else.

Will I recover from this deadness, and
Escape this numbness, and sail quietly on?
Can I take one leap and hook myself
To the movement of the universe?
And find where I can rest my head?
I will try.   I will try.

GUILT AND SHAME

The blemish on our souls
By our own invention
Of guilt and shame
Is further soiled
By unworthy ones
Who would use culpability
As a warping tool
To leverage position
And cast blemished scorn
On our child-like minds.

These empty scoundrels tinker
With our consciousness
In a way that gives birth
To valueless fault.
They depend on error
And transparent shame
And the defense of blame
That engulfs a body,
To cower a soul
And harness the unsuspecting.

The innocents who believe
Their mistake of effort
Must pay penance
In a heavy cloud of shame
Bear the weight of social disgrace
In dumb enslavement
Of mind and vision.
Shame, the invention

Of a spineless society
To enslave the populace,
In contrast to the vigor
Of joyous productivity
That exists in the absence
Of the invention of guilt
And the preposterous inference
Of censure and disapproval
That directs men to imperfection
And down the road of failing.

Dragged not by guilt or shame
The human energy of multitudes
Would generate extra love
Of sincere and bless-ed offering.
Joy would spring in all hearts l
And the enslaved mature
Would become loving again
And children would retain
Their energetic innocence.

How stupid could we be
To adopt the word, shame,
From our forefathers,
Or the word, guilt, guilt, guilt
That knows no meaning
In the gentle afterworld.

LYING TO MY SHADOW

In my soul of imaginations
I use something akin to Braille
To admit to my deviations
In the sector where I fail.

I am blinded by my scheming eyes
And the visions they evoke
A harsh beacon that will realize
A shadow as thin as smoke.

If I could see conversion
To a complete human being
Not blinded by my introversions
That will ever go unseen.

I would find a satisfaction
From my friends who call me cool
And reduce my strategies to minimum
And leave my shadow full.

HEALER

Tell me of your despair
And let my eyes
Comfort your distress.

Tell me of your fatigue
And let my conversation
Restore your energy.

Tell me of your failings
And let my whispering
Make you confident.

Tell me of your pain
And let my voice
Give you ease.

Tell me of your heartache
And let my gentle touch
Rekindle your vibrant spirit.

MEMORY

We admire the human
Who can remember so much,
His memory and acumen
And that recall touch.

But what good is history
In this attic of the mind
If life's unfolding mystery
Has been to us unkind?

So give me that person
Who has no regret.
And spare me the curs'd one
Who can never forget.

GLOW

This tiny spark o You have been given o Is all for you o
Cared for o It will forever glow. o
In the glory of achievement,
o In the turmoil of decision,
o It will guide you;

In the pursuit of mystery
The roar of excitement
The fog of despair.
This spark and its glow
Are entrusted to you
To sustain and protect
To shelter in the maelstrom
To cherish in the calm.
Its pilot presence
Will sometimes disappear
In the countercurrents
Of honor and defeat
In silence and sound.
It can be swept away,
Along with the glow

And it's up to you o To nourish it o And give it breath o
Which will ignite it o Again and again o
And mirror back its promise.

ON TOP OF IT

I see through the mirror
I can see eons ahead and I know the past
The cloud I am riding is swift and precise.
All molecules of the universe
Are focused on me.
My voice is Herculean.
My sinews are electric
I know the path ahead.
I move steady. I'm sure of myself.
I am on top of it.
Others follow my lead.
The sun shines strongly on me,
I reflect stars at night,
I invite no detours.
I operate on instinct.
My gut is happy with boldness.
My followers grin.
There is good music everywhere.
I am lucky.
My body is robust.
I breathe particles of fortune.
My friendship is rampant,
My words are believed.
My songs are sung.
Flowers flourish in my presence.
Children believe my face.
I speak all languages.
I understand the snowflake.
I teach the teachers.
I discuss the forbidden.
I am one with the mighty.
I sleep soundly and eat heartily.
All adore me and speak softly.
These may be the reasons,
I am on top of it.

"Enjoy every minute. There's plenty of time to be dead."
~ A. Whitney Brown

'TIL DEATH DO US PART

SUMMER DEATH

The arrival of November rain,
Washes the field with lesions,
And leaves the earth in pain.
It's the orbit of the seasons.

The tarnished flora knows
To put itself asunder.
Then signals the December snows
To hide the death of summer.

HOW I'D LIKE TO BE REMEMBERED

"Do you believe in an afterlife ?"
He asked me.
"A what?"
"Life after death."
"Well, er, no..." I said.
"What's this all about, anyway?"

"I heard you say, " he said,
"You'd like to be remembered
As a good member of our community
After you die."
"Yes, that's right."
"Well, if you don't believe in an afterlife,
"What does it matter
How you are remembered?"

"I'd like my heirs to think well of me.
I'd like my sperm to go into a nitrogen bank,
So my genes will be perpetuated
Into the future."

"But if there is no afterlife," he said,
"What does it matter what they think of you?
You won't benefit by it.
You won't be able to know what they think.
You'll be dead."

"Oh," I said. "I guess I do believe
In an afterlife.
Why would I care what people think,
And how my offspring carry on,
If I couldn't observe their action
And reaction
After I'm gone."

CERTAINTY

When you're down in the ground
Six feet under for keeps,
Every body has found
There's no need for receipts.

TRIP TO THE TOMBS

She was the bearer
Of ponderous weight
She could not endure.
It dug into her heart
Like thoughts made of
A Brutus blade.
She braced herself
In the unwelcome clench
Of the fire-toothed hound.
Pangs sprung from
Her twisted bowels.

She was not a Rosenberg
Not an Aaron Burr.
Her swollen shame
Pressed down on
Her sunken head.
So much that
She became invisible.
And was forever
Never seen again.

WHAT IS IN US WILL
FOREVER STAY THERE

We all know it is in us.
We do not wish to see it
Or hear it
Nor tell one another.

We take it to our end
Letting the next ones
Discover it on their own.

And so, they also
Do not reveal it
Not even in death.

FAREWELL, MY DAD

Farewell, my Dad, I say to you softly,
In a tone I have never used before.
As you lay here gasping for air,
In this sterile place of dormitory cots
For the elderly, whose only earthly claim
Is that no one knows the body next to him.
Only bodies lying supine ready for death.
But I am here, writing these lines
With the wish you could hear them
As you drop deeper into nothingness.

I know these lines will be postmarked
"Return to Sender," "Addressee Unknown."
That's been our condition these 30 years.
Your only son. We have not known each other.
I own no treasure house of cherished memories.
Father's Day is only a Hallmark invention to me.
Since your wife, my mother, died at my birthing,
My birthday has no calendar date for you.

Contrary in your life, you were reluctant
To recognize the man I had become, and I you.
But now our paths have converged,
And we walk on together, hand on shoulder.
I will re-invent you and visit your grave often.
For what is my life if I cannot have pride
In the heritage, my heritage, that you have given me?
Farewell, my Dad.

I AM MY OWN REWARD

I'm tired to the bone, my temper is thin,
I'd rather be alone and live in my skin.

No beauty am I, and I can feel it.
My face is a sigh, my lines reveal it.

As the end gets nearer and I look toward the grave,
I look to the mirror, ah! There's something to save.

Not skin nor sanity or these earthly things
Nor my temporal vanity, my angels' wings.

It's my brave soul, my protection and sword,
It makes me whole. I am my own reward.

MARILYN DIED TODAY

And so this entity
Identified as a girl
And used as a launching pad
For notoriety and lust

Will be lost to all
But her parents who mourn
That their daughter
Did not do better

Than the woman on the cul de sac
Who has two fine boys
On the honor roll
And playing football

Yes, Marilyn, you crouched
And peeked through curtains
And enticed us with your fanny
And your un-siliconed breasts,

A sort of Cleopatra, you could
Wave an arm in effortless grace
 To attract secrecy and harm
With unknowing dumb bitchness;

A sweet symbol of our decadence
A cardboard figure of promise
A collective hope
Of scheming men.

And so, the prisoner was hauled off
To the sod hole in the fields
And dumped in
Making room now
For someone else.

ORPHANS

In a world of no
abortions,
We'd be burdened with abandoned
orphans.

In a world of abortions
only,
My parents would've been mighty
lonely.

BIRTHDAYS

How old are you?
He asked me.
I dunno, I said.
Don't you keep count? He asked.
I said, Count of what?
Every year at your birthday is a year.
I don't know when I was birthed.
Don't you have a birth certificate?
Yes, I should.
Don't you every look at it?
Why should I? I know I was birthed.
But you should know how old you are!
Why?
So when people ask you.
Why are people curious to know?
They'd just like to know.
What if I didn't tell them?
Then they'd judge for themselves.
How?
By the way you look, the way you act.
They would estimate my age?
Yes, I guess.
But why do they want to know?
If you are young,
They want to treat you like a youngster.
If you are old,
They want to treat you like an oldster.
But what if I were old but acted young,
Or young and acted old?
It would be confusing,
They want you to act your age.
Why?
I guess they want to put you in a slot.
Slot?
Well, yes, they want each person
To act and be a certain way.
Why?
It's convenient. It helps them to know
How to treat people.
According to what?
According to their age.
But what if I'm 95 and feel 25?
Or 25 and feel 95?

Then they'll act toward you
Based on how you feel.
So, if I don't know my age,
And feel young,
Then they'll behave toward me
Differently?
Sure, but I warn you.
Of what?
If you are old and act young,
Oldsters will resent you.
Resent me?
Yes, old people don't want you
To act young. And --
Young people don't want you
To act young.
Why?
Everyone loses their youth.
It's natural. The world
Is a cruel place to live.
It destroys youth.
Everyone starts dying
The day they were born.
Dying?
Yes. Your days are numbered.
So, you count the days?
Yes, from when you were born.
And the higher the number,
The closer you are to death?
Yes. The more birthdays,
The closer you are to death.
So a birthday celebration
Is a gloomy event?
No. It's not supposed to be.
Why celebrate birthdays?
I dunno, It's always been done.
So, if I don't celebrate my birthday,
And, I don't know how old I am,
I don't know how close I am to
death?
Well, sorta.

THIS LAND IS MY LAND

A riddle . . .

My name is on the deed
I have no mouths to feed.

I am home at last,
No landscaping or cutting grass.

There's no mortgage to worry me
This is the pod, I am the pea.

No rowdy kids, no loud traffic
I'm no part of the demographic.

No particular view to appreciate
No location that's bound to depreciate.

I am without human cares.
I will pass this land on to my heirs.

The earth feeds on me.
And it considers me debris.

I reside in this earthly brine.
This location is totally mine.

No jewels or adornments to plunder.
I am six feet under.

It's the only thing a person ever owns
The resting place of his weary bones.

DO NOT STUDY DEATH

Let us not be impatient with death.
In the playground of our desires,
We are not privileged to know
Death's lingerings and direction.
Nor does it know its own.
Death has the physique of a jellyfish.
If we encourage it, it slides within us.
Death is a sneak thief.
Do not study it or give it attention.
It is fascinating but not important.
Do not allow it to live in you.
It, too, struggles with life.

When we study death
We diminish life and suffocate it.
If we illuminate the paperweight of death
It becomes not a beacon
But a taunter, an oppressor,
And renders us glued with obsession.
When we challenge its tin voice
And give life to this paperdoll apparition
Or serious attention to this theater mirage
The paperweight will implode.

Do not be impatient with death.
If we study death, contentment evaporates.
We need not build a textbook
Of death numbers and statistics.
Death is not the minus sign
That we assign along with our impatience.
Nor is it an entity that deserves
A chapter of our attention.
It is not an opponent nor a friend,
Neither an angel nor a sphinx.

If you entertain the specter of death,
Quickly fasten a label to it:
A panorama of awareness,
A wishing well, or savior,
A notion of regret or hope,
A birdsong of mourning,
A deep hole or pirate.
But do not study death.

Our notions of death gnaw away
At our biological structure
And our veil of cosmetics.
Let others study death.
Let them limp through life
Dragging their comrade of despair
With impatience
And thwarted desires
To their simple destination.

Death is a flawed pursuit,
An engagement unworthy.
Death feeds off human impatience.
Do not allow this visitor Death
To enter your meadow of strength
And taint the beauty of your adventure.
Death is a fiction of life.
It is an indiscriminate vacuum
That sucks blossoms of vitality
From your garden of creation.
It does not understand you.

Death is a weakling and easily killed.
If it were hardy and unrelenting
We would not be alive --
Comforting ourselves by enjoyment
And floating in our dreams,
And exhalting in our pleasures
And glowing with excitement
And reaffirming life's opiates.
Need I go on? Death has no part in this.
If we study death
These stimulants evaporate
And we are left with a coffin
Of our own making
With our fears realized
And a gravesite of welcome,
An epitaph prepared,
Where we are enjoined
To a catacomb of cohorts
Who smile at our defeat
In this ironic victory of death.

THE MISSING POEM

When your time comes and you take your last breath
You realize the inevitability of taxes and death.

Many poems have been written about death and dying
Encompassing sobbing, bereavement and crying.

In fact I've counted 34,869 death poems on dying
And could count 34,869 more without even trying.

But the important item of these miscellaneous facts is
Poets don't write poems about taxes.

ABSOLUTE POWER

The officers gave the job to Eichmann
Adolf was his name.
His colleagues called him "mouse."
He was not the embodiment of evil
As some would suspect.
He was a choirboy
The equivalent of a Boy Scout.
In fact, he looked the other way
When dozens went to the gas chamber.
He was dutiful and quiet.
Soon, his power expanded in proportion
To the number of deaths he mandated.
There's a postulate in there somewhere.

The officers gave the job to Eichmann
Because no other would take it.
They were mortified
When he became more powerful
Than they.
He wasn't a smart guy.
At the Einwhonermeldeamt in Berlin
It shows he was just dumb,
With no job, so they picked him.
God can give life, he gave death.

ENDURANCE

The assailant stabbed her
Not once but several times
And left her for dead.
Blood spread on the carpet
As he exited through the back door.
She lay motionless, but not dead.
She managed to get up.
Blood marked her path
To the front door.
She went down to her knees.
She grappled with the handle
Opened it and crawled
To the neighbor's front door
And died.

I saw these lines in the report
In the Pioneer Press
As a teenager in St Paul, Minnesota.
And ever since then,
They are pasted on the forehead
Of each eligible stranger
As I walk in the streets of St Paul
Even 25 years later.
Yes, each person will die.
Eventually, but not before
They will struggle to the doorstep
Of a neighbor.
And until then,
Each person will endure.

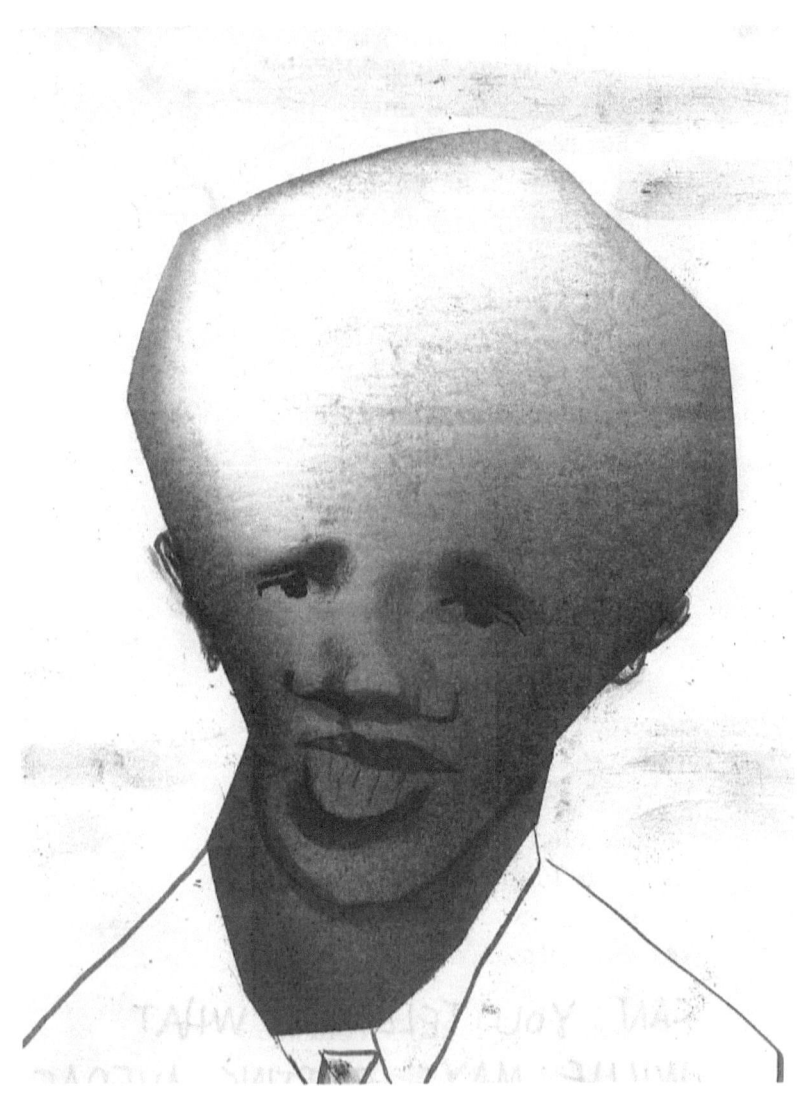

AFTER DEATH IT DOESN'T COUNT

Upon his death we have perceived
The good and unique of this neighbor man.
The recognition he should have received
Was never a part of his earthly span.

It's during existence we ought to notice
As days and decades roll along.
All during that time we should give our focus
Not when touch and hope are gone.

"The soul is healed by being with children."
~ Fyodor Dostoevsky

THE CHILDREN

HOLDING BACK

I questioned her,
This tiny girl,
Miniature and doll-like.
Quietly...
"Effrocene," she said,
And where from?
She nodded her head
To the East.
She wiped her hands
On her jeans.
She looked
At her toes
And waited for
Another question.

I thought of several,
But it was so enchanting,
The way she said,
"Effrocene."
I made an excuse
To drift on
But I turned
And smiled,
Leaving her with
Her "Effrocene."

BOY'S QUEST

Rain clouds raced and threatened, you see.
I laced up tight my sneakers, size three.
Would I dare climb that slippery tree?
Not very safe, you will agree.

The others were gathered there to see
If indeed I could climb that tree
Where on top a dove might be,
Perhaps a toad or bumblebee.

Now, being a boy of six and three
With splintered fingers and battered knee
I set upon my wish to see.
How far up I could climb that tree.

I listened intently to their plea
To reconsider my lofty spree.
No one had ever climbed that tree;
They stoutly believed it would never be.

They offered presents like sugary tea,
Chocolate milk and the pantry key,
All the color of the wide blue sea
If I would agree to abandon the tree.

Expressing a premature victory,
They went away in jubilee,
Believing that they could think of me
As one who failed ingloriously.

But I never gave in, you see.
I climbed to the very top of that tree.
Neither toad nor dove did I see,
Just the sky and another tree.

WORD POWER

Bollman folded his arms as he stared at me.
I had his attention, little me.
I told him how I had mounted a wide-winged moth
And flown to the light bulbs and back down
In our third grade classroom.
"You're just making this up," Bollman said to me.
He watched me close my smile to a straight line.
My eyes felt watery and the fuzzy hair rose on my arms.
A dribble of urine trickled in my underwear.
I swallowed, almost in a gulp, and cleared my throat.
Goosebumps appeared on my neck,
I shivered once then began to sweat.
I shuffled my feet to stop my shaking knees.
I could feel my penis shivering up into itself.
My anus tightened and shrunk smaller.
My face got warm and was getting hotter.
My breathing became faster and shallow.
And now my hands were shaking and sweating.
I wanted to put them in my mouth
And chew on my fingernails or suck on my thumb.
And then I spoke and did not recognize the loud voice
That was defending me and what I had said.
"What?" He said.
I didn't know how to repeat myself.
So I ran away.

ANSWERS

When I was young,
and being an unruly brat,
My sentences usually started with,
"I can answer that."

And now that I'm mature
and wearing a different hat,
I answer like a worthy adult:
"I do not know the answer to that."

HIS ENNUI

It is too early
For this young boy sapling
To be plagued by torment.
But the winds of awry metabolism
Have bent his boughs
And curled his limbs.

Imagined fear
Has made his torso anxious,
Gnarled and rigid.
I will release the knots
Of tension and rigidity
And make his dreams become soft
And his face become calm.

I will convey to him my love
And gain his approval.
He will rise out of his tunnel
Of bleak despair
And reach out to me
For my strength.

MY TEAM

An embryo somewhere
Will play for my team.
A mother strong as a bear.
Father of powerful gene.

This child of physical grace,
Will play for my team.
Sinuous muscle and handsome face,
Confident, proud, with self-esteem.

This child of aspiration,
Will play for my team.
Practice, work and perspiration
Energy, power and steam.

This athlete of success
Will play for my team.
We will all be blessed
By his rigorous regime.

This athlete most adored
Will play for my team.
He will come aboard.
Go! Yellow and green!

One day the best of them all
Will play for my team.
When they shout, "Play Ball!"
He will be on my team.

THE GOLD PENNY

I found the penny on the ground,
Beside my mom's new car.
I snatched the gold and looked around
And thanked my lucky star.

My brothers were not walking by,
My sister was asleep,
My dog, the only witness,
Did not say a peep.

I held the gold within my hand
And continued on my way;
I deftly held my contraband
So none could snatch it away.

I whistled at my good fortune,
That I had found this gold,
And t'was a generous portion,
For just a ten-year-old.

I decided to do some fishing
And extend my luck at the lake.
I proceeded on my mission,
Carrying my newfound stake.

A warm breeze was blowing
And the August sun was hot;
I unraveled all my fishing gear
Feeling a big one would be caught.

No one in our family
Had ever landed a bass,
So with great energy
I threw a mighty cast.

Way out to the middle,
My bait and hook they flew,

But alongside the vittles
My gold penny went too!!!

I could see my penny fly,
A way up in the sky,
And then just as high,
A big bass gave it a try!

He rose from the deep
As high as a mile,
Then swallowed my penny
With an indulgent smile!

Then coming down from the sky
He also gulped my bait,
On the very first try
Before it was too late.

I reeled him in
With hardly a struggle,
And there within
My gold was in his muzzle.

For supper that night
I was one happy lass.
With great appetite
We delighted in bass.

Ever since I was ten.
I've regaled in my glory
Over and over again,
It's become my fishing story

When two people converse,
Deception will unfold,
But that's how it's supposed to be
When a fish story is told.

THE WORTHLESS, PRICELESS, LITTLE BOY

In kindergarten
He was always in motion
And when he spoke
It was not always
Understandable by his teacher,
Mrs. Johnson, or us kids.
We made fun of it.
But he had a gleam in his eye
That said he loved you
And that you would always be
In his heart. That was fun.

The system separated us.
Me to Middle School,
He to Special Ed.
Long after, I saw him
At graduation time.
He had a beard
And it hid him well.
His destiny was not sure.

I wondered
If in his beautiful head
He still had memories
Of what a lovely boy he was.
He was worthless to me back then,
But, now that I am a parent
His memory for me is priceless.

BUDDY'S MOTHER

When we were kids
And playing sandlot baseball
I would always pick Buddy for my side.
Not because he was a good player,
But because he had a mother
Who would sit in the bleachers and referee.

You could be sure if it were a close call,
Like a tag out at second base,
All the players would look to the fat lady
Sitting up in the stands on a hot summer day
Partly concealed by an umbrella.
Buddy's mother's face would burst out
From behind the Mickey Mouse umbrella
And belt out her decision
And no one would dispute it.

One day, Clifford, who was my catcher that day,
Got up from a slide into third base
Where he was called out by Buddy's mother.
He brushed the dirt from his sleeves
And walked off the field straight toward her.
Now, since no one had ever challenged her before,
We all watched in silence as he deliberately
Walked up the seven steps of the bleachers
And stood and stared at her sunburned plump face.
He said something and then walked down
And resumed his place as catcher on our team.

As I recall that summer of '56
Buddy's mother never came to another game.
And whenever we had a close decision,
Safe or out was determined by a flip of the coin.
Years later when I saw Clifford at a tavern,
The day before he joined the Marines,
I asked, "What did you say to her?"
Clifford said he just looked her in the eye and said,
"Quit messin' with our game."

THE BANANA

It lay there on the kitchen counter
Solid and stiff like an iron ice cream bar
Still green from the grocery shelf
Not like the fake ones in the movies.

It regaled in its innocence
Its green tight skin unpeelable
With promise of voluminous vitamins
And healthful minerals not yet ripe.

"Don't eat it," she said. "It would hurt your tummy."
"Besides, it's for your father."
24 hours passed, and no father ate it.
The banana began to ripen.

"I told you it was for your father."
She saw me examining the brown specks.
"Where's Dad?" I asked
She turned on the TV and didn't answer.

It was now 24 hours more and the banana knew it.
It was more brown that yellow
And rather than straight as a soldier
It was puffy and brown and soggy.

"Where's Dad?" I asked, 24 hours later.
"You can have the banana now," she said.
"But where's Dad?" I asked.
She turned on the TV and didn't answer

DISCONNECT

I am the child you dissolved.
The one who would be Beethoven,
Or Jeffrey Dahmer.
My eyes can still see,
And my fingers can reach.
My tongue is swollen
But still available for sound.
Yes, I do exist and I am real,
As real as your temporal pursuits.

I reside here in Saturn.
I am a part of a blue ring
And watch you from afar,
Alongside my fellow beings.
We do not grow or shrink.
We remain the same,
As we are remembered.
Always sort of smiling.

KNOWITALL

When I was small,
Say, ten years of age
I read a lot and listened a lot
And pretty soon
I knew all that there was to learn.

As a youth I went off to school
And studied hard
And got good grades
And I learned a lot
And pretty soon
I felt I learned
All there was to learn.

Now, as an adult
I am going downhill.
I'm playing catch up.
I not only have to learn what's new
But unlearn
What's no longer true.

I wish I were a child again.

THE VASSER STREET KIDLETS

The melodic cry of laughter
Swells from the armpit
Of the Vasser Street garbage dump.
Kids in clothing as tattered
As torn labels from tuna tins
March about in frenzied circles.

These gleeful kidlets parade about,
Banging on Teflon pans,
Buzzing wax paper melodies.
In the darkening dusk.
They turn and disappear behind
A rusted, red, Rocket '68

And reappear in communion garb
In procession, proud and deliberate
With polished patent leather
In solemn candle-lighted steps
With mournful Gregorian tunes
They shift and glide
Through the alley, into the night.

DAUGHTER DECENDING STAIRS

I have always lived in a one-story house.
Ranch-style they call it,
Sometimes a rambler,
That's a better name.
My parents seemed to ramble
From one house to another.
Always a one-storier.
As a kid, I always thought houses were one-story.
No gables, or widow's watch, or cozy attic.

In high school I had a girl friend
Who lived in a two-story house.
On our first date, when I went to pick her up,
Her father called up, "Cynthia, he's here."
Like in a movie, she descended the staircase.
Lightly holding on to the banister,
The kind that kids would slide down.

Someday, if I ever get married,
I'm going to ask my bride,
"Would you like to live in a two-story house?"
And then I will explain how it will be fun for the kids
To run down the stairs to see what Santa brought,
Or for me to call up to my teen-age daughter,
"He's here !"

THE TOY DRUM

As a child, I grew to be an elder
And as an elder I grew to be a child.
Now that I am a child again
I know the sound.

I discovered the sound
When I crawled inside my toy drum
And listened to the empty oxygen,
The tone that only I can hear.
I did not allow the composition
Of board, metal, and skin
To interfere with the composition
Of the sound in my toy drum.

I lay there in peace, alone.
Like on a Sahara evening
With the full moon rising,
Watching the beams reflect off the sand
And bounce in the distance, the heartbeat
The footbeat, the drumbeat.

They marched above me
Invisible to the eye and in darkness moving
All to the same thrumming rhythm
In natural cadence.
Coming in recurrent waves
Lifting me and delivering me
To where I had begun,
Knowing the sound
In the inner chambers of my toy drum.

HOW KIDS LEARN

A Yellow Jacket bit Jeri on the arm.
She was talking, smiling when it struck
Tears came to her eyes
And she cried out in pain.
I tried my best
To suck the venom from her arm.
I felt sorry.
She was on her way to the Creek Store.
"You'll soon forget it ..."

Later that summer afternoon
Watching our humming bird saucer,
A Yellow Jacket alighted on the edge
And then waded into the crimson syrup.
I watched as he waded in deeper
And then attempted to retrace his steps,
But to no avail.
His wings fluttered until exhausted.
His spindly legs tugged in despair.
He rested, upright, and tried again.
Was he aware that a member of his clan
Had hurt my Jeri earlier in the day?
Probably not. But insects are smart!
Look how a bee can find its way home!
No telling what a Yellow Jacket can do.

Maybe scientists already know.
The Yellow Jacket was gasping now.
A mosquito landed near the saucer;
I thought I saw him smile
To see such distress.
Yellow Jackets eat mosquitoes.

When I was young,
And we used to play soldiers,
I was always made to be the German,
Because my name sounds German.
(It's Norwegian.)

The other kids attacked my fort
Often, and always victorious.
Sometimes they shot me as a spy.
Once they tortured me in the lake
To get some secrets.
Once they tied me to a tree
But I escaped.

Jeri came back from the store.
"I showed off my bite."
Everyone had a remedy.
I laughed and pointed out the
Yellow Jacket in the saucer...
Dying in crimson, sugary glue.
"Can't you help him?" Jeri said.
"Why?"
"Well, because."
"But he bit you."
"How do you know he bit me?"
"He's a Yellow Jacket isn't he?"
"Yes, but I don't think he's
The one who bit me."
"No matter. They're all alike."
"But why torture him?"
"Because one of his clan bit you."
"What good ? Why kill him?"
"It'll teach him a lesson."

"He bit Mom," our son said,
"Kill him, Dad."
"Shouldn't you be doing your
chores?"

*"Music washes away from the soul
the dust of everyday life."
~ Berthold Auerbach*

THE MUSIC

MUSIC IN BRITAIN

In the Elizabethan Hall in London
Seventeen persons in chic black
Wedded their talents into Mendelssohn
Proper and accurate, the technicians
Were errorless. The swell erupted
In the mode of Sibelius
And well reached my Three Pound Sterling pew.
Mendelssohn would have been grinning.

I left at mid-break for an Irish Pub
On the opposite side of the river
Where two weathered partners,
One with plaintive fiddle
And the other with Segovia skills
Washed a message of scorn and sorrow
Over we, the clean and unharmed.

Three pints later I was in a blues bar
By the same name or something like it
Closing my eyes and trying to imagine
That a New Orleans accent
Wasn't coming from five Brits
Who honorably played the correct notes
But strayed from the experience.

We each hear our own melody
And we each talk our own talk
And together we become a human voice
And let music be our touch.

SOME OF THAT JAZZ

I speak musically with my cats,
Punctuating new phrases
And monopolizing long paragraphs.
Those who dig, scratch for more.

The itchy rhythm flows through me.
My saxophone renders flashes
Of muffled sounds and riffs
Like pheromones from birdsong,
As my fingers scamper over
The worn-slate keys.

I don't complain and don't explain.
I leave my language at the escritoire
And settle back to commoness.
To scratch this perseverant itch
Until it stops.

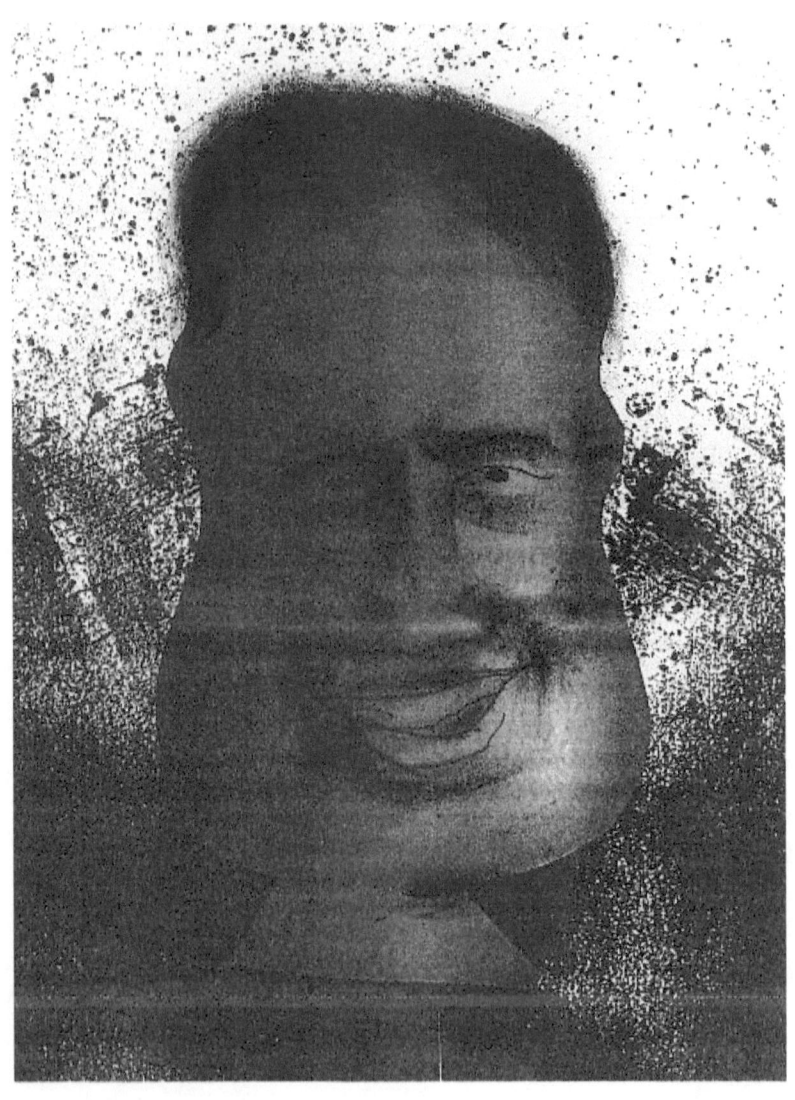

TENOR SAX

Coleman Hawkins woke up this morning
Not knowing
This would be
The most important day of his life
In terms of his effect
On Humanity.

He placed his tenor sax
In its case
And took the streetcar
To the recording studio
Where he and five other fellows
Made jazz.

The melodies have since
Disappeared in ether
But Angels have accepted
One of them into Heaven,
A solo on tenor sax called
Body and Soul.

NOTHING NEW

I cringe to hear musicians who are willin'
To imitate the style of Bob Dylan.

And please don't presume to attack and bomb us
With poetry sounding like Dylan Thomas.

What's the world of creativity coming to?
Where can we look for something really new?

Will it take a genuine Aboriginal
To give us something that is original?

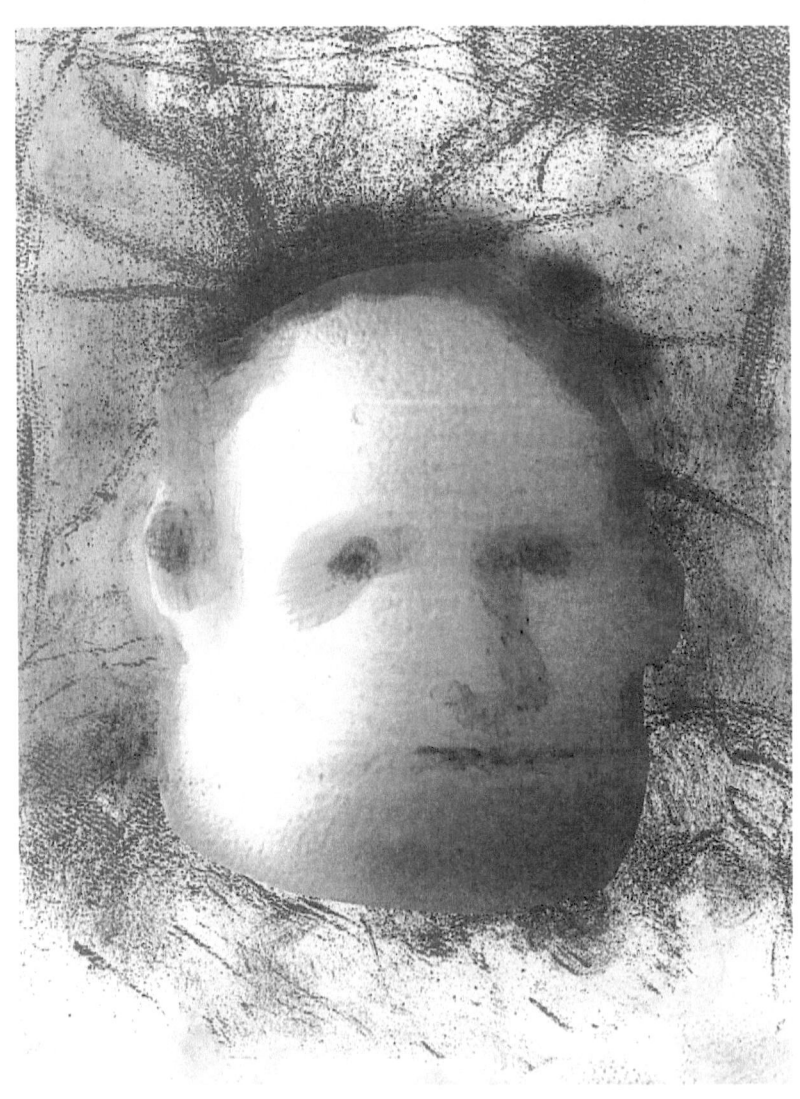

PREJUDICE

Why would anyone want to play a harp as their choice of musical instrument? You are too limited. You can't play any fast music. Popular songs don't sound right on it. Certainly not jazz or blue grass. You have to sit down when you play. And what if you're in a wheel chair and only have one hand? And you could be black.

DEMOCRACY

Democracy won't work.
A dissimilar audience
Listening, humming, singing
Trying to keep time
To John Phillip Susa
Or the Horst Wessel Lied
By foot tapping
And hand clapping...
Will always
Fall behind the rhythm.

THE ERA OF RADIO

It was a choice between
The Sears radio
And a puppy.
My parents chose the radio.
But as I look back now,
Jack Benny, Charlie McCarthy,
Fibber McGee and Molly, and
The Great Gildersleeve,
Taught me wit and respect
In my early-teen years.

The announcement of Pearl Harbor
Struck us when we arrived home
From church on December 7th 1941.
In '43 the Green Hornet thrilled us.
While Mom was cooking supper.
In '44 "I Love a Mystery" brought intrigue.

At night the mature programs aired.
Upstairs our bed was next to the floor grate.
My older brother and I listened to
"The Lucky Strike Hit Parade"
And we learned the latest tunes,
And of course, the benefits of cigarettes.
The Andrews Sisters, Bing Crosby,
Frank Sinatra and Perry Como.
Poetry we couldn't remember,
But we could remember the words,
To hundreds of songs.
The Era of Radio - I lived through it
And learned the audio pathway to imagination.

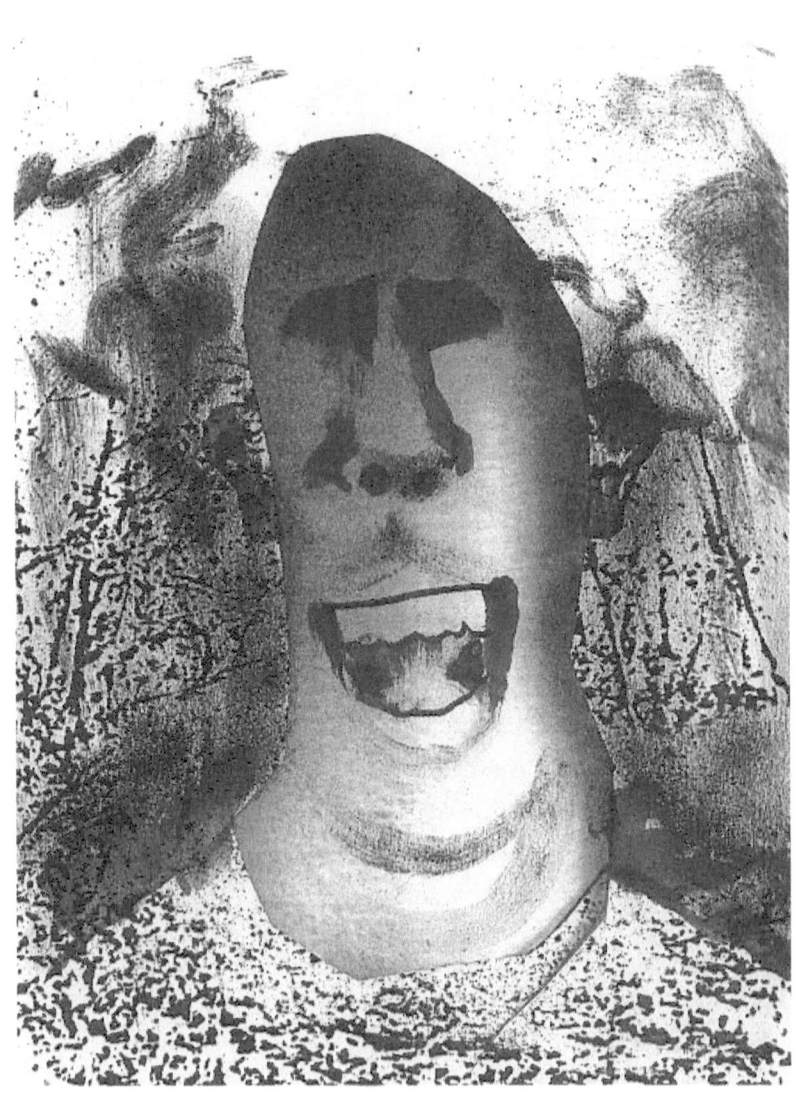

I WILL FIND MY WAY

There is something more than this.
Must I behold the indignity of fools
The snickers of nincompoops?
I haunt their miserable domain
And augment my mundane routine
Of confetti and ticket stubs
Sprinkled with humiliation and threat
I who is laughed on and spat at
The recipient of scorn and rumor.

Beyond this street corner
Around this curve in my road
At the end of this wicked path
There is a place where I belong
Where my toil will be rewarded
My kindness be returned
And my beauty be recognized.

No hall of mirrors . No more.
No misdirection or faulty voices.
Until I am breathless and tattered
Exhausted and unkempt
Gaunt and emaciated,
I will walk on and walk on.
I will find my way,
To the music of realization,
To the glory that awaits.

THE TAP, TAP, TAP

Scribes write of its beauty,
Melody that eludes,
All knowingness, all rhythmness.
It cannot be found in the ether.
It escapes all gene recognition.
Pythagoras described it,
Alanis carries it on.

It is always right, never swerves.
Always there, the beat, in our dreams,
In our quiet contemplations,
In our moody reflections.
Tap, tap, tap the melody goes,
Even Thelonious knows
When it is not right.

Ancestors knew all this.
It separates us from other animals
And keeps us vibrant and charming.
No discord can make it righter
No exotic beat can make it sweeter.
We are content and proud
To persist at this higher echelon.

It is there, not to be learned.
It is known and to be used.
We cannot destroy its cadence
Or divert it.
We can only live it.
The tap, tap, tap
Sings to us in its rhythms,
Clear and true resonance.

MY MOTHER'S PIANO

Things are not going well with her.
She's playing the piano.
She always plays her piano in mid-afternoon
When things are not going well.

Since I was five years old
I've known.

She would begin playing.
I would crawl underneath
The Steinway
And lay there
Alone in the sound
Magnificent
Close my eyes
And let the sound enter my body.

The music would swell
Banishing her hurt.
Vanishing her melancholy.
Together, we let
The world disappear
To the music of Rachmaninov.
And then she would make supper
Smiling.

WHY THE MUSIC OF FRED HERSCH IS RIGHT

Music like all matter
Is the result of the Binary World
A Plus here, a Minus there,
A Black note here, a White note there,
Some Energy here, great Energy there.
A pulsing, waiting to be heard.

When music is created,
Circles of tonal warmth waft from
The instrument played upon.
The pianist presents what we
 call music.
Others would call these
Electrical tensions of sound.

A kitten on a key board
Can form these vibrations
But they are entertaining
Only to other cats.
But here is why the music
Of Fred Hersch is right.

He makes mistakeless music.
And his secret is this.
He splits each atom of warming tones
To explode into particles of sound
And combines this fine powder of
 neighboring notes
To assemble resonant sound units.

These synchronous elements
 of resonance
Form a strong string of vibrations
 and pitch
Of binary offs and ons
Of black keys and white keys
That Hersch can decipher for us
As a song , as music, as celebration.

Now this explanation may
 seem abstract
And downright bodacious to some
And musically disconcerting
 to scholars,
But Hersch says the music is
 out there
And it somehow filters through
 to him.
Listen. You will know that he is right.

WANDER WITH ME

Let us find ourselves again.
Let us go
Beyond the mortar of this road
That weaves and bends
In ribbon style
To the music of our heritage
To the songs of our ancestors.

Instead, let us release ourselves
From the bindery of history's diaries.
And erase the pages of the past.
Hold my hands in yours.
Let our footsteps be guided
By our own cadence.

While others roam their rigid highways
Come with me. Head high,
Our hearts will bear the burdens
Of unpleasant interruptions
Of painful barriers
And we will emerge unscathed
In oceans of auburn meadows
And find ourselves again.

THE BEST IN THE
WORLD

On a quiet Sunday
Alone in the music section
Of a vacant Wal-Mart morning
I listen to the voice
Pressed into plastic
Thundering from the speakers.

In simple Italian.
Bellowing with fervor,
Pleading for love and *rispetto*.

No male voice better,
Now, before, or forever.
Captured in audio magic for the ages.
It's the best in the world.
Operatic excellence.
This voice, and me alone.
I am honored
And give my *rispetto*.

He could be emoting these very lines,
Or orating a radio commercial,
And still you would thrill
To know it's the best
In the world.
This privilege,
On a quiet Sunday.

*"It is easier to lead men to combat, stirring up
their passion, than to restrain them and direct
them toward the patient labours of peace."*
~ Andre Gide

WAR AND
TURMOIL

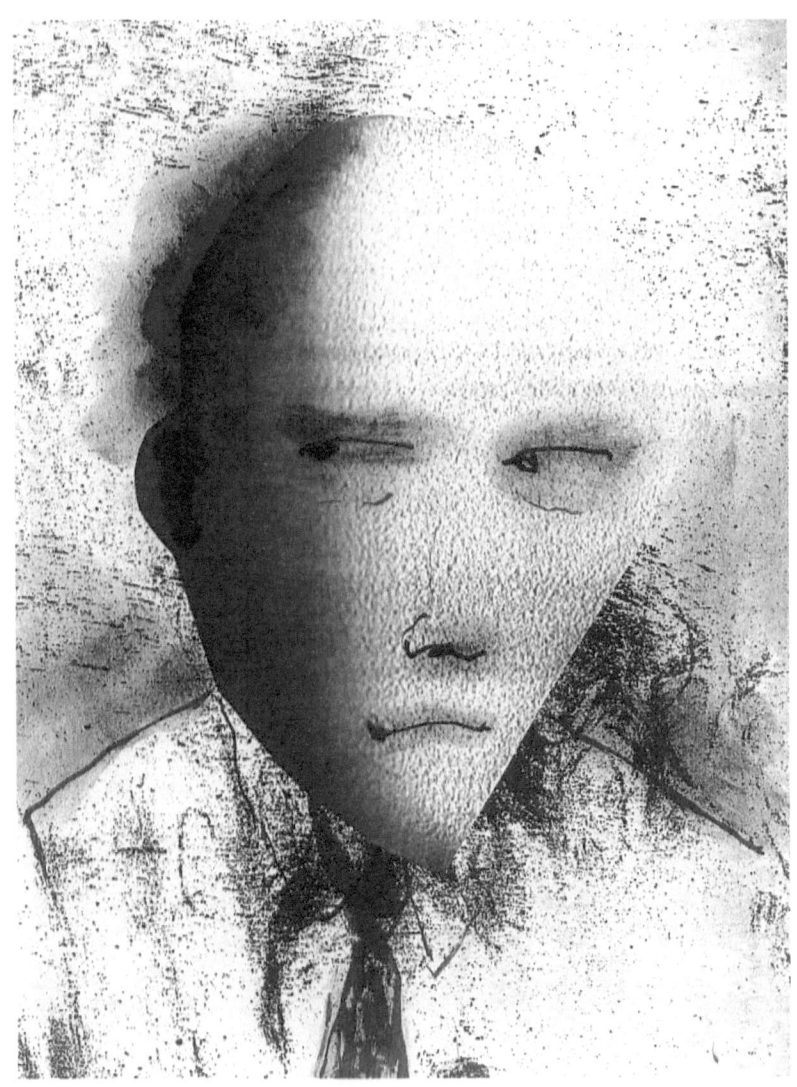

THE CAUSE

I have known
This folly of his.
For I have passed through
These same catacombs
Where glory dwells
In stinging bites
With dragons spewing hollow slogans
And feeding on the blood and flesh
Of unwary youth.
And their cash register of dreams.

I was his commanding officer.
I regret that, and I regret that
"The Cause" sucked me into this maelstrom,
To ascend giddily
To a so-called higher station
Where both he and I would achieve
Swift and sure stature,
Noble judgment and esteem.

Life is not precious,
His face said to the world.
A mere volunteer, he -
He would surrender his body
To the delicious destiny
Of "The Cause."

He died unnaturally, with no glory.
Not like I would have wanted him to.
But historical lies will right this wrong.
His memory will be etched in family granite
And endure in fantasy and folktale.
But I will carry this nightmare
Of righteous bond to "The Cause"
Forever, within my calendar pages.

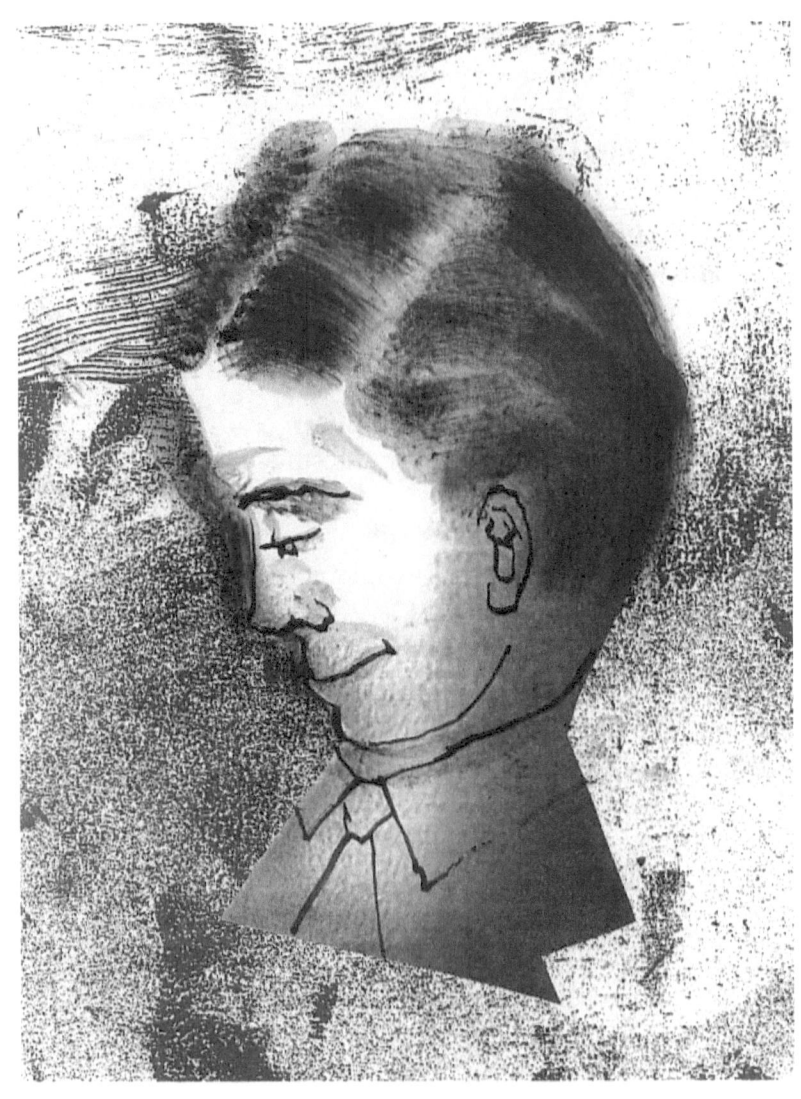

ALONZO

The video man
Holds heavy camera on weakening
  shoulder,
Emergency helpers streaming from
  building,
Avoiding collapsing debris.
Out of the smoking WTC,
And cloaked in grey dust
Comes Arabian-looking figure,
No doubt Puerto Rican,
Or exchange student.
Video man stops him for interview
And says.
"What's going on back in there?"
"Not good."
"Are you scared?"
"No, I just came out to get air."
"Who's still in there?"
"Many."
(cough, cough.)
"Are they hurt?"
"Many."
"Like?"
"Some have fallen down stairs,
Some trampled, some gasping."
"Have you brought any out so far?"
"Three so far."

"Are any dead in there?"
He nodded, wiping dust from eyes
With smoky handkerchief.
"Are you going back in there?"
"Yes, I have no choice."
"Are you scared?"
"No, goodbye."
"Wait, what's your name?"
"Alonzo."
"From?"
"Brooklyn."
Alonzo walks the long block
Back to WTC.
On his way, borrows gas mask
From a fireman
And enters North Tower again.
Three minutes later
The North Tower collapses.
His name was Alonzo.

WAR LORD

I grant you, I never intended fame.
Born of plain tastes of the plain;
And of normal academic energy.
My father arranged for free matriculation
At our country's highest military school;
I had no dreams of military glory.
I learned the trade as quartermaster
And began an undistinguished career
As bookkeeper of uniforms and arms.

The stench of blood came to me first
In my father's butchery, a noted tannery,
Where I was known to have leather skin.
Next came patriotic human blood.
Skirmishes with Indians and Aztecs.
Glory for my nation.
Fate then sent me to the western wilds.
To learn both military boredomand alcohol
Which caused a break in my Army career
Until an event of the unity of our nation
And I was granted a commission anew.

No skill did I own except dedication
To the idea that prisoners are not taken.
That war is war and killing is the contest.
My battle record is my legacy:
Kill or be killed; no quarter for the meek.
I walked among strewn bodies.
I stayed the course, victory at any price.
The enemy was brought to its knees.

They named me Attila. Or, Napoleon.
I wanted to retire from the military
To a plain house on the prairie.
But the tides of political expedience
Thrust me to a White House in the capital.
I grant you, a President I am not.
The enemy continued its undermine.

The country continued to divide.
Intelligentsia and scoundrels
From within my own camp
Became leeches to peace and accord.
Confidence, disguised as guidance,
Again alcohol and cigars
Were my counsel.

As a puppet I was granted
The rewards of fame
And as a war hero to lively parades.
Upon retirement from my octad
Of the Presidency
My fame expanded abroad
Where I traveled and lectured,
Lunched with Caliphs and dined
With Victoria.

Back in my homeland
I retired not to the plains
But to the greed and avarice of
Metropolis
Where scoundrels again
Promised me wealth
Only to grant me shame and
A public whipping.

Left for me is to write these lines,
They are memoirs of a man
Of the plains gone East.
Of a non-soldier beyond expectation.

I lived a surprised life.
Grant me no mausoleum.
I earned what I did
With my leathery skin.
Nothing more.

MY GUIDE

The level ocean drinks all waters from the landscape,
The earth core belches and spews its excess,
The electric clouds deliver wind and rain,
And man, a bird born wingless, is there to receive.

Let us kneel to Him who will show us enlightenment,
Who will show us the path of rightness and speed,
And proclaim benevolence and promise,
Who will give us fulfillment and comfort.

And one day, He will appear from the Eastern mist
Bearing documents of steel and words of supplication.
And in unison we will raise our salute to our Guide
Wearing in pride, an armband of The Swastika.

IN A MOMENT

In a selfish moment
I took my classmate's crayon.
I begged forgiveness.

In a greedy moment
I robbed my mother's purse.
I sought forgiveness.

In a thirsty moment
I swiped my buddy's soft drink.
I asked for consideration.

In a fanciful moment
I stole a stranger's car.
I asked for a second chance.

In a enraged moment
I crippled a neighbor's son.
I asked for clemency.

In an angry moment
I killed my girlfriend.
I pleaded temporary insanity.

BRAVE GIRL WANDERING

Before full daylight
Just at the top of the enemy ridge...
I see her tall silhouette in my gunsight.
She paces the horizoned hills
Of no-man's-land,
Rifle lowered in candid confidence.
Just... the outline of her body...
Her head is raised skyward, whispering to the dawn.
Her moving figure reveals a captivating aberration...
To the other side, she is the cunning panther.
From this view, she is a pet kitten wandering.
Yet, she is knowingly explosive.
I wait and watch her delicious gait.
Possessing her, I hold my fire...
She turns and drops out of sight back to whence she came.

I KILLED A MAN

In thunder and horror and mud I spent
A nightmare of time in the Orient.
An echo, a beating of piercing sounds
In my brain, still battled, still abounds.

In all my waking hours these days.
I still haven't figured out this maze.
I try to believe it's a gaggle of dreams,
But they just won't disappear, it seems.

Here's the episode I always recall.
It was '69 in late summer or fall.
Our outfit as usual was misaligned
A night scene that plays forever in
     my mind.

My patrol advances through human
     stench,
With sweating brow and gut clenched.
The walking dead become even bigger.
In infrared on my mental trigger.

I see a soldier approaching defenseless.
Who can be bolder, or more senseless?
He has no battle-ax, no spear, no bow.
Obeying his duty, he moves so slow.

Innocent, he comes upon my screen.
He's not much older than a teen.
My finger wobbles, I hear the sound.
His helmet bobbles, and he is down.
Did I kill a man who had no
     armament?

(I only shot at his enemy garment.)
No sour pleading, he fell to his knees
To the ground with mournful wheeze.
No response from anyone above.
I've switched my allegiance
From hawk to dove.

They shipped me East to go home
     and settle.
A hero's feast complete with medal.
It's been seven years and I'm none
     the better.
I can't bear thoughts of my Asian
     endeavor.
I've denied my allegiance to the Corps
I've denied that I engaged in that
     foreign war.

At home I've a friend who is also aware
A Vietnam Vet. We were both there.
We don't talk of the red, white and blue,
The Ho Chi Minh Trail, or of
     Dien Bien Phu.

He's a fellow veteran I always pray for,
He's my paraplegic next-door neighbor.
His praises I often sing.
I'll tell you his name; it's Hyn Thi Nyng.

THE GYPSY

He wore a coat and tie and shaved everyday. He carried a briefcase and his shoes were immaculately shined.

But this is where it ended. He was a Gypsy.

"Appearances," he would say. "That's all that it takes. Illusion -the 'real' world is the unreal world. Today is the only day. Tomorrow? Never heard of it."

In his head, he was industrious. In his body he was lazy.

"Why should man spend any time at something he doesn't want to do?," he would say.

"No, I don't steal or take anything that is not given to me. Charm, charisma...that's what the world wants from me. I give it and the world pays me back with favors. I take them because they're offered to me with good will. "

He had no home, at least not in the sense that you and I think of a home. Where his head met the pillow was his home for the moment.

His brow was unfurrowed, he followed the constraints of no external doctrine; he roamed with composure.

I once saw a woman eye him on a busy city street. She moved to walk within his aura and was satisfied just to be there.

The horizon was his. Memories were not. No scrapbook, no Internet address, only the open road.

We will never know what became of him.

SEMITE BLOOD

The familiar gunpowder stench of war
Filled my bedroom as before.
The sound of enemy voices
Were outside my teenage window.
And there I lay trapped by a heavy beam
That pinned my arm to the mattress bed
And crushed my bedside table
And the framed picture of my boy friend.

Once again I was a bedroom prisoner.
This time I was ten years older.
My breasts were full now.
My arms and thighs were mature.
I would be ripe fruit for the enemy
Who now roamed our village
As they had done ten years earlier
Harvesting the teenage girls.

I lay there listening to my breathing
Reminding me I was a cherry in autumn
At the end of a branch, the last chosen.
By my discoverer.
My breathing proclaimed the enemy
    would come.
He would be the first to partake of me
And that I must make glory of it.
A first and last enjoyment of new
    womanhood.
That he would come. I would accept him.

A warm breeze was coming through
The cracks of destroyed plaster walls
Making soft whistles.
I lay there several hours, in ragged hope
As the light in my shattered window
    was fading
And the rumble of war subsiding for
    the evening.

In my room decorated now with figurines
That once gave me comfort.
In the final evening light he arrived.
Expressionless and aware that I was
    waiting
For his tribal pride and conquering duty.
He removed his helmet
Revealing a handsome face,

A small gift fulfilled in this theater
    of shame.
And submit I did, surprising him quietly
As his camouflage wrapped me
    In foul odor
Of men he had brutalized that day.

Projecting metal splinters of armor
Came between him and me
Pressing on my body indiscriminately
So much that I did not know
What was humanly him.
The sanguine fluid of my first privacy
Flowed out richly, melting into
The maroon stains on his khakis.
Completed, exhausted, he rolled away
And stared at nothing on my white
Hovering ceiling and fell asleep.

I lay there like a cadaver in waiting,
My arm still pinned by the beam,
Drifting between terror and slumber
Unthinking of him or myself.
In a nether region, I drifted off in trance.

When I opened my eyes
He was gone and I was alive,
The cruel thunder of war had moved on
But not the seed of his visit,
That remains today
In the form of a swarthy Semite boy
Whose olive skin,
Jet-black hair
And green eyes
Are reminiscent of former ancient days
When no formal religion
Divided our Semite pagan blood,
When our roots
Were beyond historical horizons
And our tribes,
The enemy's and ours,
Were one.

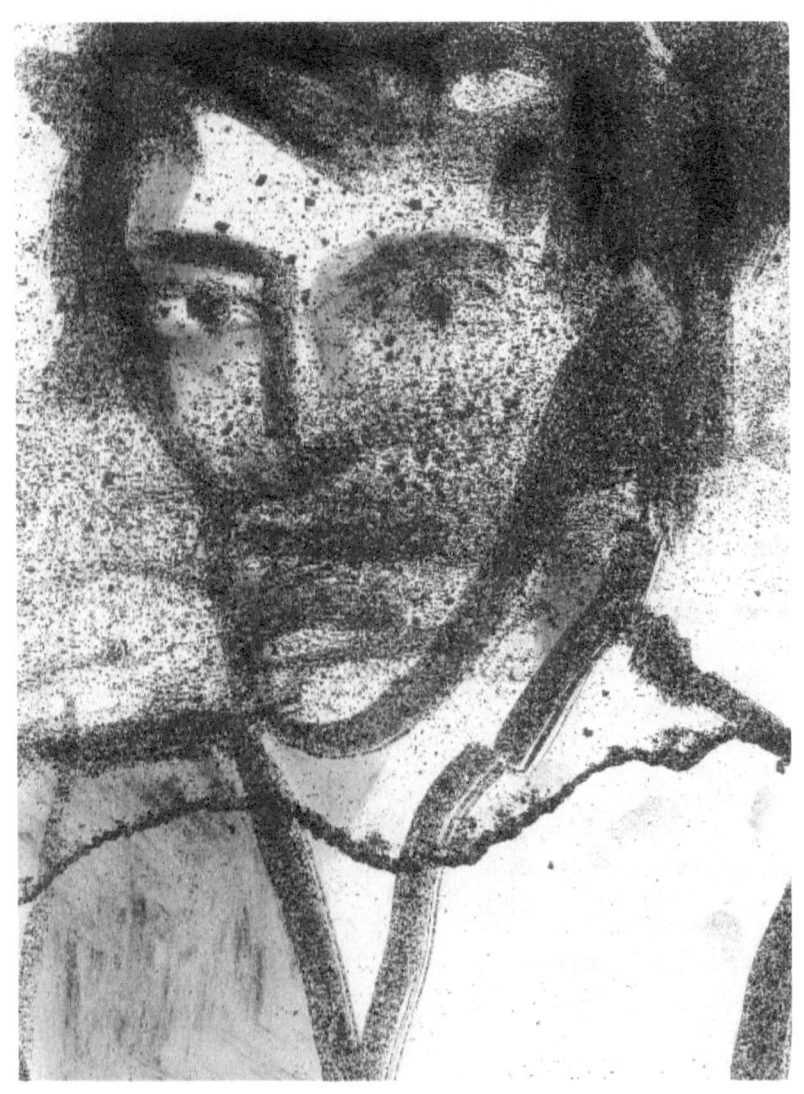

THE HUNTER

Proud was he,
In bloodstained dungaree.
He looked to be about 23.
I came upon his secrecy
As he stooped behind the maple tree,
A rifle his artillery,
Leaning up against his knee.
He worked upon his treasury,
A fallen deer in custody;
Performing backwoods surgery
Where hunting takes on rivalry,
Where poaching is utility.

A beer can raised aggressively
"This buck -it tried its best to flee,
"He got no hurt from me,
"I gave it no brutality,"
He said in gleeful victory,
Assuming a pose of bravery.

With rifle pointing now at me.
I gave him guarded courtesy.
Not about to disagree
Nor play the role of third degree
Nevertheless I could see
His kill was definitely not a he
But a slender doe in pregnancy,
The embryo cradled in her cavity.
No hero me. Cowardly,
I left those three.
The hunter, the doe, and the fawn-to-be.

TRUST

Ah tangy indulgent Trust!
You cannot be predicted or
    forced.
A fleeting perception to be wary
    of,
You flexible, transient being,
Worming your way into my
    pocket
As an afterthought, a
    happenstance.
Trust! You should not be trusted.

Does that say you do not exist?
Trust is a zephyr that
    only…existed.
We cannot demand it or expect it.
It is a summation of
    circumstances.
The hapless one being trusted.
Has vacant obligation
To trust in return.

You are an invented word - of
    what good,
If we daily obscure your
    intentions?
We look both ways to find
    to whom
And to what we should entrust
Your faulty glue.
I would be the first to never say,
"Trust me." Or "In God I trust."
    This being truth.
A decision to trust is perilous.
Based on luck and
    presumed ideals
We indulge in trust's supposed
    existence

And are saddened by breach of it.
The person trusting pays the fee,
As spectator,
    not manipulator.
The hapless investor in trust
Believes in an indulgent return,
That sadly withers away in
    fickle time.
You, Trust, may say I am
    untrusting.
But I have seen and tested your
    blindfold.
Hope is one of your wares, your
    snares,
That moral chain to capture and
    hold
Another whom I hope for or
    demand,
Believing your noose of
    encirclement
Will deliver the faithless one
    to me.

To the inexperienced,
    broken trust
Is an earthshake, a shock
    that reveals
The teetering monument of trust.
Trust puffs away like floating
    feathers,
Aimless and hollow, ignoring us,
Leaving us minus faith, blighted,
Resolved never to trust again.

THE INVISIBLE THREAD

In skimpy Montgomery Wards bathing suit,
The plump man strolled the crowded oceanside beach,
Jollywhite bellybutton hanging out.
Someone said, "That's the Archbishop of Baltimore."

In a fiery gasoline blaze ignited by his adjutant,
The Fuhrer of the Third Reich
Disappeared into cinder, mustache and all.
Only a bullet slug remained.

On a 1945 summer day in Kitakyushu-shi, Japan
The emperor deity, dressed in ceremonial robe,
From the magic of radio, spoke to his countrymen.
It was an ordinary human voice.

2 SPACESHIPS

We visited the spacecraft observation park,
Me and my little sister, on that day
In September 2001. And anticipated the launch.
Two spaceships were poised for flight.
I remember it so well.
It was my birthday, five years old in 2001.
September the 11th.

As scheduled, a bird flew by
And pinched the North spaceship.
And shortly after, a second bird
Pecked spaceship South.
The smoke and aroma of burning fuel
Grayed our observation park.
And we squinted upwards.

Against the cobalt September sky,
The tall, stalwart spaceships
Rocketed in glistening harmony and glory.
But some of the astronauts in the spaceships
Decided not to go and leaped out.
They floated strangely to the ground.
And then a loud protest came from the spaceships.
A sound like the beginning of the earth.

I embraced my little sister and held her ears.
The once clear bright day disappeared in thick soot.
Fire sirens celebrated the blastoff   -boom !   -boom !
Music of bagpipes brimmed over into the smoke,
The whistling metal made the park trees quiver eastward.
Racing people with terrified faces dashed past us,
Knocking me and my little sister to the ground.
We struggled to our feet again. Everyone was running.
I squeezed my little sister's hand and we ran too. . .

GOD'S WORD

Like a trail into a diaphanous jungle
The lone path leads aimlessly upwards
Through mist and into clouds.
I stand before the entry gate, alone.
Motionless, quiet, I stare
And then lift my hand
To touch the cold metal of the portal.
Effortlessly it swings open.
I hear my footsteps moving onto the path
That follows now over smooth pebbles
Around a bend and still skywards.
Above, I see, shrouded in mist
The cloudy form of a structure --
The kind illustrated in children's books,
Intriguing and hypnotic.
I mount the path.
No guide to instruct me.
No familiar forms nor clamor to greet me.
Only vacant and hollow sound waves.
I arrive at a final gate and enter.
Cautiously I move forward
Into structures that have no meaning (to me).

-after a few moments-

The sound came from one of the walls
Without windows nor ceiling.
It was a pleasant, or maybe unpleasant, voice.
Not unlike I would imagine a beetle speaking,
Or a rhinoceros, or butterfly.
I listened for a minute, or was it an hour?
I waited for a sign of instruction
Maybe days, trying to decipher the voice.
Alone I waited for instruction
And I remained there forever.

COME WITH ME TO LIVE

Come join with me, resolve your longing;
Fulfill the quest of all your yearning.
Come live with me where sighs conserve
The quiet and serenity of my serene preserve.
Where no intrusive corporate sound
Can soil the pleasure I have found.
Where avarice is forever denied,
And only hearts like ours reside.
Come with me where no ugliness rails
Against sweet goodness; where peace prevails.
Where tyrants and bigots recoil with fear
At the sound of stillness they cannot hear.
Where sham and shame cannot endure.
We will live and love, in our home secure.

"Life must be lived as play."
~ Plato

MIRTH, WIT, JEST, AND COMMENTARY

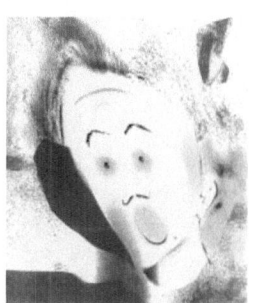

TUESDAY

Mondays are days for vigor and vim
Trying to escape the doldrums you're in.
Chances for fun are mighty slim.

Tuesdays are best for pleasure and play.
The dishes are done, so come what may.
Tuesdays I'm lazy and like it that way.

Wednesday is always the chosen date
To address all things that cannot wait,
Those items you've left to procrastinate.

Thursdays, most of us will agree
The best programs are on TV,
If you partake of such debris.

Fridays for most are seventh heaven,
They're o.k. if you're twenty-seven.
And have the stamina to last to eleven.

Saturdays are always for errands that matter,
The shopping list grows and keeps getting fatter,
Like chauffeuring kids and all that clatter.

Sunday delivers you welcome vitality,
Allows you a moment of spirituality
Before confronting Monday's reality.

Though I'll take Tuesday for my choice,
I say this with confident voice:
I like them all, and in all I'll rejoice!

AS THE WORLD TURNS

The same old thing
Used to be the new thing.
But if there's nothing new under the sun
The same old thing
Is a repeat of an old thing.
So there was only one new thing.
The first thing,
Onetime ago.

So, is nothing unique,
Unless it's an old thing?

What we need
Is another new thing.
A really new thing.

THE BIRD THAT ATE THE CAT

When I opened the screen door today,
A bird walked in, cocked his head,
Looked me straight in the eye and said,
"I ate your cat."
Then he spit out some fur,
And part of a tail, out on the kitchen floor.
I could swear that bird smiled at me.

It made a bird sound,
Stepped back as if to say,
"There! Don't you admire me?"
I was too dumbstruck to answer.
Then it said, fluffing its feathers,
"I wish my mother were here.
She taught me how to catch cats."

THE BUG

Here I am lying all flaked out.
I feel a bug with a prying snout
Trespassing me all about.

As it explores with quiet clout,
I am concerned, no doubt.
I'll lay still with nary a shout.

As it moves toward my ear
Its centipede movement I can hear.
Let me tell you what I fear.

The bug -it thinks it is my guest!
What'll I do if this pest
Down in my ear it stops to rest?

ALARM CLOCKS

I don't appreciate that godawful shock.
As you know, the culprit is the clock.
Blissful slumber shattered, killed
Nerves joggled, jolted, spilled.

It does my psyche grievous harm
To suffer hits from that alarm.
I've been scheming since adolescence
To reduce that thing to obsolesce.

Today my dream has now come true
And I can start my life anew.
No longer will I be annoyed.
That wretched thing has been destroyed.

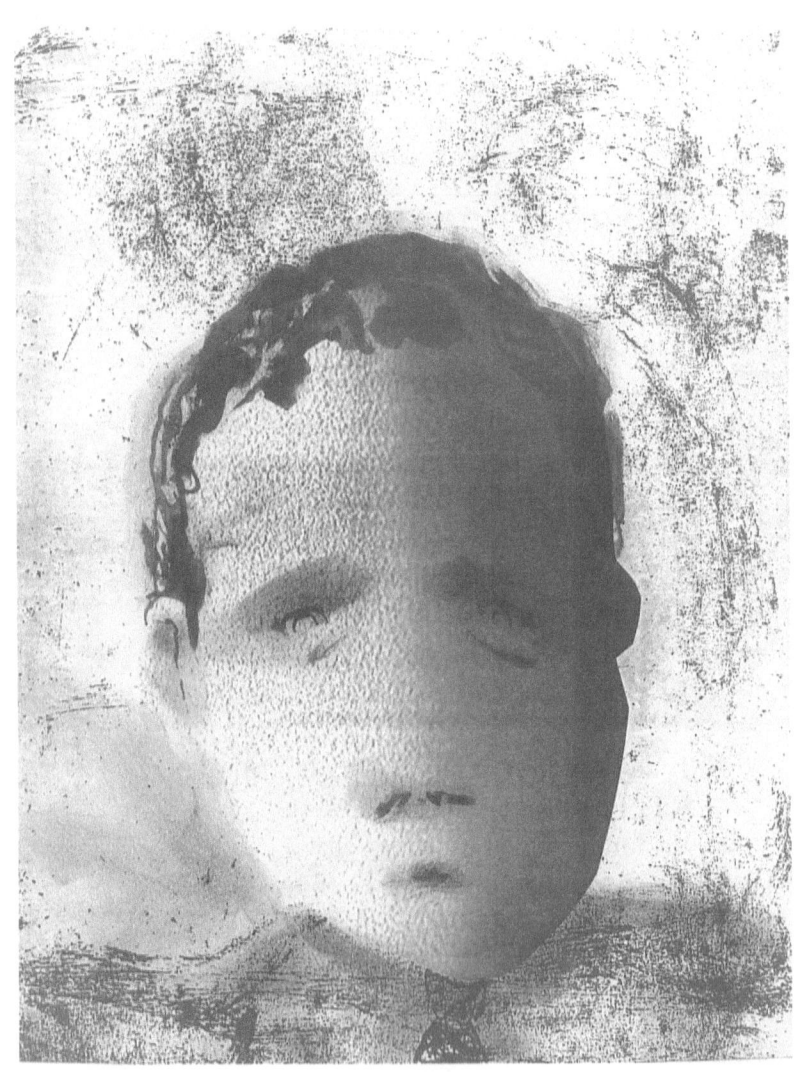

RELATIVITY

When I contemplate degrees of pain, I
    think of pain by a certain number.
At number ten you can really complain, at
    rest, in action, or even in slumber.

And, if say, the bicep is at number two, is
    the pain related to a person's size?
So here's the question I propose to you: Is
    the larger man going to agonize?

Lincoln and Washington were long of
    limb, and Hitler and Napoleon were small.
Is the pain of a taller person much more
    grim, and for tiny, tiny people none at all?

ENDINGS

Must all writing come to some end and diminish?
In truth not all lend themselves to a finish.

Whether lengthy or terse, with quiet or clamor,
Must we wrap up our verse, browbeaten by grammar?

There should be a choice as to finish or not,
To cease in the middle, or just never stop.

It would be amusing to have no end
All the more mystery to the message we send.

When we've got their attention and just stop flat
And fail to mention in the middle that

-- 30 --

Fini

EXTERMINATION

Through the magic process of mutation
A cricket grew to the size of my cat, Buddy.
It had long antennae and soft brown eyes.
And when it started eating from Buddy's dish,
My big brother said, "Let's keep the bug
And get rid of Buddy."
And my sister cried, "No!"
And began crying.
But my brother, who was bigger than both of us said,
"The cat must go."
"But why? Why?" my sister and I said,
"It doesn't even have a name."
"We'll call this thing, Buddy," my big brother said.
"But it's not a Buddy, it's just a big ol' bug," my sister said.
My brother looked at the big ol'cricket
And then looked at poor Buddy,
Who was cowering under the sofa.
And then he realized he couldn't get rid of Buddy.
My sister smiled and said, "Can we keep both?"
"No," my brother said.
"What will we do with the cricket?" I asked.
"We'll have to destroy it," he said. "Help me step on it."

EIGHT HOURS

You shouldn't lay down for eight hours straight.
To this I attest, it's a grave mistake.

Sleeping too long is action misled,
You'll regret those hours you've stiffened in bed.

With body unmoving and all stretched out,
You awake all right, but you can't turn about.

You attempt to rise with head like a balloon.
You figure you won't even make it 'til noon.

You creak to your feet and get help from the wall.
One step is a treat, while you fight not to fall.

Your eyes they won't focus. You shuffle and stumble.
Your limbs don't react, they're about to crumble.

There's no mistake, both ears are ringing.
It's not the birds. It's your head that's tingling.

When next you retire, recall what I've said:
"Eight hours is too long, to stay in a bed."

CONTAMINATION

I have this notion, as I write these lines
That I stir up emotion and unwelcome signs.

It's word-knaves like me, who write lines like this,
Who pollute our surroundings and cause us distress.

There's no absolution for my weak analogies,
My feeble locution and my frail apologies.

There should be a movement to do something about it.
Can you offer improvement? How can you allow it?

I can't face reality, as you can see.
When it comes to banalities, point the finger at me.

OVERLOAD

This Age of Information, much to my delight
And to my great elation has given me the right

To test the thin capacity of my cerebral sense,
And lucid flexibility, to remember whence

Came numbers, names and faces, as well as mental lapses,
Of figures and of places, that pass through my synapses.

Opened and unnamed, with proper impropriety
Making me untamed, in this informed society.

Will I go insane with such an overload of facts,
In my fragile cerebellum before it finally cracks?

Let me in conclusion say that you will n'er regret
When one day you discover that it's o.k. to forget.

Dear reader, rest assured that you can always prove it
Like surplus stuff on TV, you can quickly lose it.

MOSQUITO LUNCH

Famished frogs and birds and fish
Prefer dragonflies for their dish.

Hungry dragonflies like to munch
Upon mosquitoes for their lunch.

Then who do skeeters eat with glee?
Unhappily, it turns out to be me !

THE ITCH

When I scratch his back
My dog keeps switching
  and   twitching.
I think he's trying to tell me
Where he's itching!

ACCENT

Be wary how tinsel people
  address you--
From PBS pundits to
  Michael Jackson.
If you're worth it, and they choose
  to impress you,
They're sure to take on a
  British aksont.

THE GREATEST INVENTION
OF ALL TIME

The perfect wife,
Can anything match her?
My nomination :
A backscratcher.

WORRY

What, me worry?
Occasionally.
Well, yes, often.
I've been known to worry
That I won't find a way
To stop my worrying.

RISE & FALL

To me it's really amazin'
That most people... *rise*... to the
occasion.
But then comes a turtledove
And what, --they ...*fall*...in love!

APPETITE

My boy friend used to remark,
"I love you so much, mulatto girl,
I could gobble you up like a shark."

Why did I think this a lark?
Because he'd never tell me what he liked,
The white meat or the dark.

FLIGHT

I've often wished I were a bird,
To have such freedom of flight.
Unlike my trust Thunderbird
I'd soar to such great height.

On second thought those birds of feather
As mighty as they try,
Inconveniently in stormy weather
They are grounded, they cannot fly!

DIAGNOSIS

My doctor said he had the
 impression
That I was suffering from
 depression.
Well, I certainly did feel blue
But, it turns out I had the flu.

IMAGINATION

To laugh at a fat lady is
 certainly rude
But to imagine her nude is
 certainly lewd.

STARK

Life on earth is rather stark
When you consider - - -
1/3 of our life is spent in the dark.

CHANGE

When life seems spinning
 out'a control
And you haven't decided upon
 your goal,
It's time to change the toilet
 paper roll.

FAME

When you're famous your life is
 not your own.
Your life is public, your family,
 and home.
The problem with fame is you
 lose the game.
If you happen to get famous
 just change your name.

BELLY LAUGHING

Man has a talent for
 something unique
Confirmed by F. Scott at his peak
Laughter, it's called, not faint
 but hearty,
Try it at your next cocktail party.

ARGUABLE KINDNESS

H.L. Mencken, the lovable
 curmudgeon,
Once said that on his gravestone
He would like to have
 emblazoned,
"Wink your eye at some
 homely girl."

I hope that I would never be
The recipient of such kindness.

PRETTY

What could be more pretty
Than a wide-eyed little kitty?

DOING DISHES

Doing dishes most will agree,
Decidedly it's no pleasantry.
It's one of our mostest, greatest hates.
So we've resorted to paper plates.

FOUND IT!

When your contact lens falls to
   the ground
And you holler, "Dammit!"
But within just seconds it has
   been found,
The saints and devils of heaven
   and hell
Suggest you yell, "Un-Dammit!"

POETRY

Poetry comes persistently
To me like in a repetitive dream.
But always inconsistently
Like the chocolate in chocolate
   ripple ice cream.

JANUARY SALE

I love to buy things
And adore to try things
And call them my things
And don't understand why things
Can cause such writhings.

HOUR GLASS

My egg timer stands in elegant glass
As shapely as a Spanish lass.
The sands flow in it smoothly
   with ease.
Even upside down it doesn't cease.
But a fault it wants to hide,
It's useless lying on its side.

SPILLAGE

We were all told our planet is round
That's what Christopher Columbus
   found.
The earth may be round but the
   ocean is flat.
If you were a fish you would
   know that.
Ask the whales as they're
   swimming about.
If the ocean weren't flat, it would
   all spill out!

MOSQUITOES

Melodious mosquitoes are so busy.
Do they ever sleep?
If they do,
I bet they sleep without a peep.

FIREFLY

You know what'd give me fright?
A lightning bug that could bite.

TRUTH

Life would be better if I only knew
Which of the versions of truth is
    true.

GUNS

We decry the plunder and rape by
    the Huns,
Yet approve the making of bullets
    and guns.

ETERNITY

People stretch and people yawn
As life on earth goes on and on.
Stretching and yawning will go on
    and on.
      And on.

RETIREMENT

If there's one thing
    "retirement" is needing
(And it's a fault as large as the
    Andreas):

It's more time to get around
    to reading,
That picture book about the
    Himalayas.

HURRY

Should I get unfurled
By people who worry?
I'd like to live in a world
Where's it's a disgrace to
hurry.

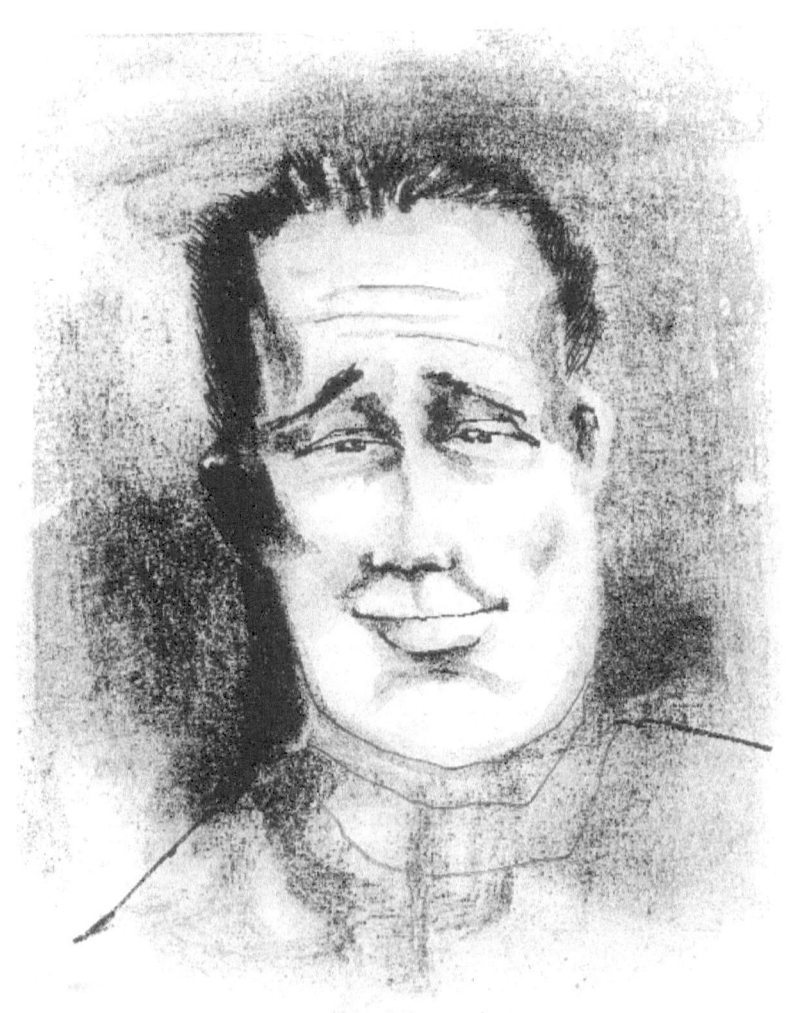

THE ANSWERS TO LIFE'S BURNING QUESTIONS

Who knows?
The Shadow doesn't know.
Certainly not my cat.
Who knows?
Maybe Elvis or Picasso?
How 'bout Jefferson?
Now here's who should know:
Your barber, bartender or big brother.
The Internet doesn't know.
Pope John Paul didn't know.
He said so.
So did Mother Teresa.
Walter Cronkite didn't know.
My professor didn't know.
He proved that.
And Mr. Nielsen didn't know, either.
Nor did Governor Dewey.
My grandfather didn't know.
I used to know, when I was 13.
I'm looking for someone who knows.

*"If a woman hasn't got a tiny streak of harlot
in her, she is a dry stick as a rule."*
~ D.H. Lawrence

FLESHTONES

SWEET SKIN

Females come in different dimensions.
Their appearance begets my intentions.

Some women are of heavy limb,
Others are lithe and pleasantly slim.

Some men like a dainty physique,
Sparkling eyes and rosy cheek.

And for m'lady fair
I prefer curly hair.

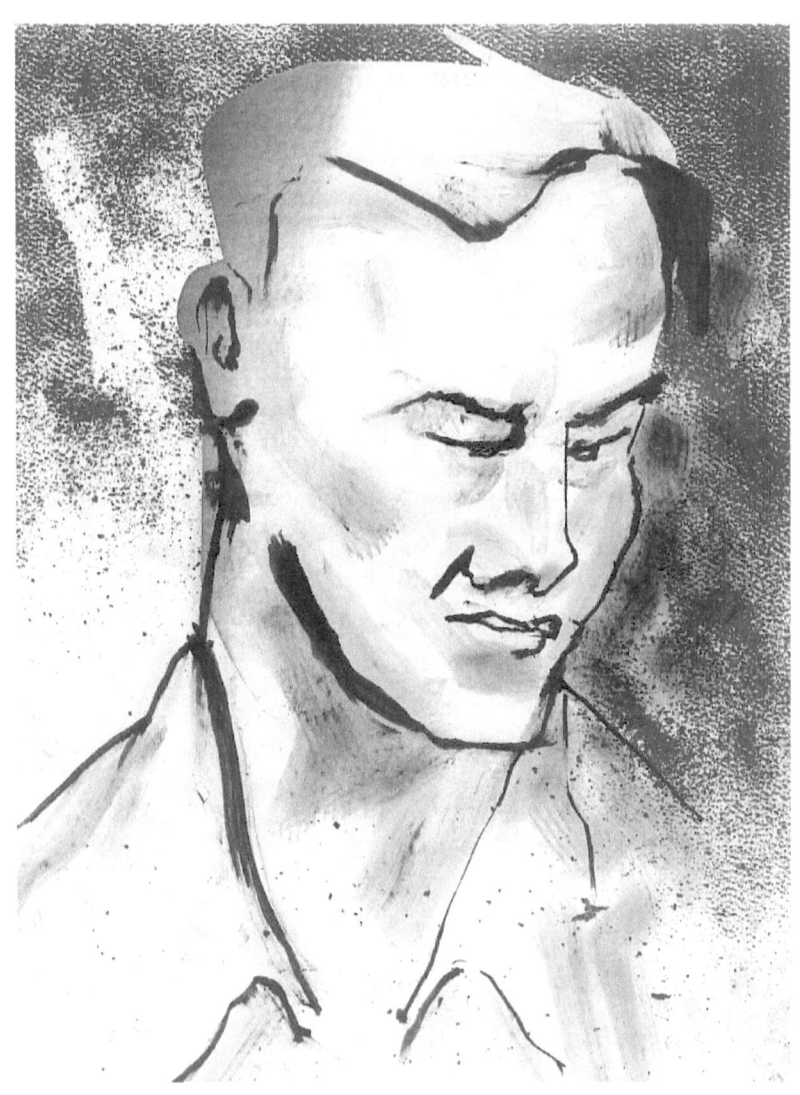

THE VIOLETS

The faint rays of the early summer sun
Searched the tall quiet pines
And found us on our warm night blanket,
Peaceful in our nakedness.

You in repose and me in recline.
I gazed at the summer ceiling,
Watching the final star fade in the dawn.
A morning bird announced the new day.

Bathed in dew I spotted a violet blue
Your favorite flower and I fetched it.
But a petal fell before I reached you.
My prize for you was incomplete.

You smiled and pointed to another,
Where a profusion of violets were budding.
I brought you a bouquet and placed them
In the soft fold of your breasts.

You smiled as I rearranged them
With my finger and my tongue,
Listening to your heartbeat,
Caressing your nipple with my cheek.

We fell asleep as the morning sun rose.
We dreamed of violets and summer nights
And the pleasures we bring to each other
In the quiet of the pines.

THE PHOTOGRAPH

She asked me for a photograph
Of me, hair combed and nude.
And it was the right thing to ask
For I was leaving that day.
I knew what she wanted -
A picture of the bliss I had given her -
Better than a first kiss
Or a taste of melted chocolate.

She wanted an eye-pleasure,
A delicate morsel of memory
Of me (and once her).
That moment of bliss experienced
That may never happen again,
Not exactly like this..

And today, somewhere, a faded photo
Of forty years ago
Resides perilously between pages
Of an unremembered book
On an abandoned shelf
Lost almost to memory.

I am a bliss giver. I am aware.
And I receive bliss in return
But I do not need
A photograph to remind. No.
For the bliss that I give,
Like a transgender being,
I give to myself.

THE REQUEST

All my life
I had spent unhappy moments
Pursuing the social graces of
Fitting relationships.
My virtues were transparent
To would-be suitors.
Men, that is,
Who, according to Fairy Tales
And Children's Books,
Should be attracted to me.
But none came.
My scorebook was empty.
My affections unfulfilled..
Until one day
In my late 30's
I felt a firm touch on my shoulder
And turned to find
A gentle smile
On the face of a woman
Much plainer than I
Entreating me to come to her
And nestle my sorry head
In her bosom
And suck of her goodness.

THE GARDEN OF FRUITS

No rational move or moment was involved.
She moved at me with the pace of a floating leaf.
No intention implied, just filaments of whispers
That covered me with appeals.
I, not my body, responded with unheard murmurs.
The touch of her finger on my shoulder
And then my hand on her limbs gently.

No meeting of iris to iris was involved.
All of this in seconds, and then we were entwined.
Time, the great inhibitor, was destroyed.
In lastingness we lay in pronation.
Softly we entered the human garden of fruits,
Devouring our succulent findings,
Like in a birthing channel,
Submitting to a force beyond ourselves,
Not knowing where we were bound.

No spoken words were involved.
If there were language for this,
The finger of knowing would touch us each
And implore silence, lest we become translucent.
Unaware that all of this would come to an end.

MY BEAUTIFUL BODY

My beautiful body.
I must hide it
From intruders
Who would steal an image
Of me naked.

My beautiful body.
I must repress
My keen sense of sexuality
And relegate it to my diary.

My beautiful body remains detached
Unappreciated by others
Who would compliment me
And my beautiful body.

My beautiful body.
I live in dilemma
And betray my delicacy
By shifting my immodesty
To feigned virtue.

FEAR

He told me he was leaving
And I better not follow his tracks.
He was enraged and seething
As I watched him through the cracks.

I'll forget his quiet abuses.
Those macho actions he revered.
Fear is useless,
Unless you are the one being feared.

THAT INTERIM ENCOUNTER

She carries a parcel
Bought at a trinket store.
She left a donation in the penny jar,

This woman who arrives quietly,
Passing through the membrane of my musings.
Absent are any terms.

I rapidly taste the scarlet blossom
And fondle the stamen lobe
Until the color rises.

The misty condition motions yes,
The signals certain my direction,
I find comfort in her being.

This one only who requires no denials,
And huuuummmmms a melody untiresome
With notes whimsically flat.

We wash ourselves in the raven river.
Sparkled lightdrops pepper us,
We hear hushed voices, up the stairs from below.

We enter back into the requirements
With faces strong and brave
To continue the battle bold.

THE ASCENT

It seemed the right thing to do.
A warm sun beat on our shoulders
A breeze came from the west.
We headed up the path
Into the hushed woods.

The crackle of twigs
Broke the thoughts of the moment
That was to come.
She pursued the trail
And like a resolute deer
She followed her desires
With resolve to be with me.

I paused at a level place
And my eyes said,
"Here would be good."
"No." her glance returned.
We moved up the next hill.
Through a place that was steep,
She needed help climbing.

I placed my hands on her thighs
And pushed on her cheeks.
She turned and took my hand
And gave it a quiet kiss.

I stopped and grasped her limbs
Putting my hands again.
On her firm hips.
I slid one hand lower.
She kissed me again and
We continued up the hill.
To a light spot at the crest.
Underneath some lush vines
We nestled into a bed of leaves
And spent the warm afternoon.

LIFE'S LARGER LEDGER

They dwell somewhere in my body,
Like flicks from a motion picture film.
Or fragments of a dream
From life's larger ledger.

Their playful prods overtake me
As I stroll to the top of the hill,
The cool summer breeze at my brow;
They toast my inner folds.
They entertain me, sparkling a smile.

Like sunrays from a departing cloud,
Or spiraling leaves in a September gust.
These morsels of recollection
Are all mine for private moments,
Resting and teasing, napping and pleasing.
My private theater.

They linger, fade and then depart.
They retreat but not to retire;
They live on in vapors of memory.
In my ledger, they reside.
And visit me again.

VISITOR TO THE REALM

Of bread, this I sing.
The calendar pages
On the wall,
Flutter onward
Relentlessly.
And each season
Slips to the next,
A constant search.
The calendar pictures
Like me, inwardly.
Lusting for bread.

These robust pictures
Have eyes
And a taste for scent.
To learn what is not
And to taste what
They shouldn't.

Down the hall
She stopped at the elevator
To wave goodbye,
Only to prove
She had someone to
Wave to.
Glancing at her cell,
She moved on,
Hungry as I.

BESIDE ME

The moon rises tonight at 9:42 p.m.
The sun rises tomorrow at 6:23 a.m.
Only these two will I know as true
In my coming dreamless hours,
As I lie here with you.

Your breathing caresses me,
Heralding the coming rain,
Sometimes like flurries of snow.
You are beside me,
This I know.

I notice every movement of your body,
Intrigued that you are faintly mine.
I can hear the night bird sing
Morning is coming.
What will it bring?

DESTINATION

How long must I endure
These walls of discontent
That bar the promise
Of that sweet flow of warm
Lovefluid that melted us into one?

It's been six years now
And I'm slipping further down
Into this dusky housestrife chasm
Peopled with lifeless familiar faces,
Disappointment on each brow.

Tattered memories in a scrapbook,
Stale aromas of endless drudgery,
No gate to open or path to follow.
No spare energy is left
To comfort this shell of a woman.

Yes, I have been tempted
By the music of affectionate glances,
And the lubricant of tender touches,
The warmth of indirect suggestions,
The play of body throb,
And the dreams that come after.

But why repeat the cycle?
My existence is wholly mine.
I have chosen the mortar
To form my life anew
And now I must garner the clay and grit,
And discover the discipline to make me strong.

KNOWN   FRUIT

Ma soeur, of the same blood,
You have blossomed
Like me, two years ago
Into a beautiful being.
From the same loins
Of the same beautiful sires.
And we are here, together
In the same blood
Mixing, mixing, mixing
Of the same blood
Ma soeur, ma soeur.

We have found outlaw beauty--
Me, the desperado
You the scoundrel, the rogue
With your cheeks of rouge
And your thighs of oak
And you're plump breasts
Betrayed by no boy, yet.
I am the first to taste you
The first to eat upon your
Tummy down.

We are one and two
And you make us three and four.
Ah! ma soeur.
Let us continue on into the twilight.
And pass through this veil of bared secrets
Down unexplored paths.
We who are blossomed and unknowing.
We have tasted nectar that few have known.

THE DANCING GIRL

Like a flower petal lost to the wind
Or a kitten's eyes nearly closed,
The dancing girl looks and grins
And lights beside her nearly-betrothed.

Up again swiftly to other ether,
Her essence spins with lithe ambition.
He fails once more to quickly seize her
Before she continues her airy rendition.

Her arms move softly in sweet directions,
Her body sways in luminescence.
Her limbs invite such warm affections;
Her movement expresses a loving essence.

He lumbers heavily to gain possession
With hands that defy her grace and elegance.
She pivots from his awkward aggression
To continue alone her mystical dance.

From time eternal a suitor tries
To believe the magician's wine;
Even a petal or kitten's eyes
Can never touch the divine.

To another world she rapidly flees
To locales he will not understand;
He pleads in remorse upon his knees
For her to accept his wedding band.

But wrapped in clouds she continues her dance,
Her soul is engaged in seeing
A light new world of great expanse
That breathes her very being.

A PLACE INSIDE OF ME

As a child, I found
A place inside of me to run to and hide.
When thunder would come
I would curl into my softness
Inside of me,
Until all beyond had rumbled away.

Do you remember the day
Once while strolling the ruins
I came upon you,. in the rain and wind?
I guided you into my hiding place
And we curled into this softness.

Now when thunder threatens
My softness beckons.
You may still run and hide,
For I am here
To welcome you to your place inside of me.

"They do not love that do not show their love."
~ William Shakespeare

HEARTFELT

I NEVER SAID

I never said I could write lyrics
Or understand the blindfold of Wallace Stevens.
I never said I could sing a song
Or reach the range of Lena Horn.

I never said I could swallow the beauty of a rainbow
Or reflect on the essence of a Modigliani.
I never said I could pitch a baseball
Or surpass the speed of Don Dreisdel.

I never said I could graft a flower
Or rediscover the methods of Burbank.
I never said I could get along with other humans
Or comprehend why you chose to love me.

I KNEW HIM AS HUSBAND

I knew him as husband.
A once-young husband,
Carved into my reverie,
Never to escape from there.

Yes, I have changed
But he hasn't.
His appearance deluded me,
Especially when he delighted me.

Near the end, it was his smile
That turned upside down
Others would tell me,
But I did not see it.

So, now that he is gone,
The grave is dirted over,
I see him still in those reveries
(We always called them that).

No one can have him now.
My memories are mine
Not to be shared,
Only by me.

HORIZONTAL   LIGHT

At that time of day, just before twilight
When the sunrays slant horizontal,
Skimming their light across the flat landscape
Defining the lone Nebraska trees,
These were the moments that he remembered.
When she was beside him, crossing the grassland
In his vintage two-seat purple pickup
On their way to the Crimson Roadhouse and Bar.
Tugging down the brim of her baseball cap,
Her lips tightened as if in pleasure/pain,
Squinting into the hard horizontal sunlight
That accentuated mascara lines around her eyes,
Traced a penciled outline of her t-shirted breasts,
And re-warmed her sunburned cheekbones.
He would be counting the minutes until they were sipping
A welcome cold beer at the countryside dance hall.

It only lasted one spring and summer.
His letter to her in the Fall was returned undeliverable.
But the recollections of that horizontal sunlight
That required her to pull that visor over her brow
Stick in his memories these many years later.
When he's out baling hay or delivering a calf
Or mending a fence or branding his cattle.
In those same horizontal rays just before twilight
That cause him to pull down the brim of his own cap,
An apparition floats momentarily in his head,
That has no meaning and no connection to his helpers,
His three sons and teenage daughter,
Who pull the brims of their baseball caps down too,
Just before twilight on the Nebraska grassland.

I KNOW

I don't wear a watch,
But I know what time is.

I've never read a novel,
But I know what a story is.

I've never said, "I love you."
But I do.

SHADOW RHYTHM

As we walked
Together
That first time
Our shadows, separate,
Long in the afternoon city-
Our rhythm
Began to emerge.
I sensed a familiar
Timing…pulse
I listened intently-
The taught skin of
My temples tuned
To those vibrations,
As our pace quickened
And our shadows merged.

WAITING

There is a cherished sound I recognize.
It is not that cat in the next apartment
Tumbling objects on a vacant afternoon.
Nor is it the muffled Eastern language of the neighbor
Nor the air conditioner grinding out
Its music of comfort to a weary me.
It is a sound more human
And lovely.

It is her footsteps.
She has promised to return today.
I am impudently casual
And then I turn impatient
And I wait,
Impulsively with my heart to the door
To hear her footfall from the elevator.
I recognize the
Seventeen magical steps
I wait, and then
Casually open the door ajar
Just slightly
As if I didn't expect her so soon.

VISITORS WELCOME

No one comes here much anymore.
I live too far out in the country.
My mistake, to get away from it all.

My mailbox flag is rusty and noisy,
After a fallen snow there are no tire tracks
In my driveway, or shoveled path to my house.

No knocking at my door or neighbor visits;
I shouldn't have invested in an unlisted phone.
No barking. My dog, Ranger, died last winter.

You left. Not of your own liking, nor of mine.
A victim of that planet plague of AIDS.
Although your faint voice I can still hear.

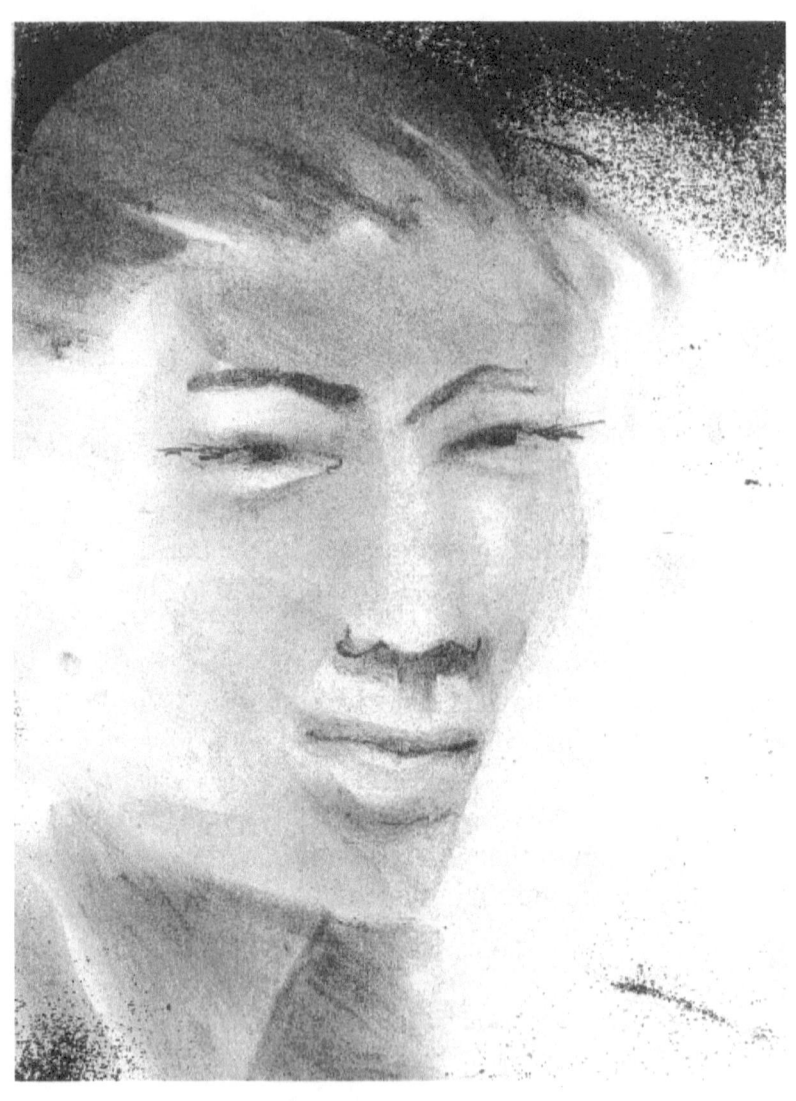

NO WORD FROM HIM

He said, "I'll write."
And my faith
Was failed again this morning.
Among the Tuesday missives
Of color and clamor,
Were no words from him.
Among the windowed envelopes
And gay matters of trivia,
There is no word from him.
I wait here in this prairie
To listen for his footsteps,
To once again
Press his heartbeat.
Will his word come to me?
What can I expect?
A cancelled stamp would be sufficient
A blank page would do.

THE WOMAN FROM IPANEMA

As she walks down to the ocean
In her usual strolling motion,
I recall her from years ago--
Maybe forty or fifty or so--
In her bikini so fashionably cute,
What some call a bathing suit.

Back then I hoped she would look at me
As she moved silkily toward the sea.
Her saunter needed no explanation.
She captured my youthful imagination.
Her stately pace caused me to purr.
My desperate dreams were always of her.

I would devour her feminine stride
As she walked on toward the tide.
My fantasy was never rewarded
(Nor could my bankroll ever afford it).
Dreams were pleasure enough for me,
A raw young man of fifteen and three.

But now such years have passed,
My eyes no longer are glassed.
I'm left with secret reminiscence
Of that young man's fragile innocence,
And the reality from too many years
That life holds less than it appears.

HURT FLOWS OUT OF ME

Hurt flows out of me
When I am touched
By the warmth of your hand,
When I am bathed
By the murmur of your gentle words.

I bruise myself by my own doing;
I am felled by my own hearing
Of voices, distant, approaching --
Voices clambering and clanging --
Speaking of me.

Off in the forest of my head.
They repeat my name and yours
And I rush to find you
To let hurt flow out of me.

YOU UNDRESS MY MIND

I have written like Shakespeare
And Christopher Marlowe, too,
But the words I own that are so dear
Are the words I receive from you.

Most words you speak are not spoken,
They are cloudless and kind.
My eyes they have awoken,
Your words undress my mind.

MY SOUL IS MINE

I've stood my ground,
Drawn a circular line.
Within this circle round
I'll keep what is mine.

You have my heart
You've taken it whole.
Now we're apart.
I'll pay the toll.

My heart you can steal,
But this remember
I know my soul
You can't dismember.

THE VACANT ROOM

In my soul there is a room
That you have occupied all these years.
I have held you in esteem
As a friend, as essence.

Yes, you are gone, never to return to me.
Your existence is in a new form
Scattered among others in the universe
Where your spirit is recycled once again.

Shall I now search through my closet?
For an anguished veil of black
And drape myself in sorrow
And crouch for days of mourning?

I think you would prefer me not.
But instead fill your vacant room
With precious possessions
Of memories of you and me.

We will move on.
The invisible you, close by,
A presence beside me,
Cheering me on.

THE LOG

Just you and me
We two
Left here in this
Quiet hollow log.
No falling leaf
Disturbs our peace.

The planet shifts
And rumbles by
Disappearing beyond.
We watch.
Only we remain
Quiet in our log.

Soft snow covers
The spruce and elm
And blankets
Our warm abode.
December winds
Shift and whistle.

Plump drifts
Of virgin snow
Muffle us
For the season
Of sleeping.

BY THE WAY

By the way, it was your sweetness that
Attracted a young me to that room
And drew me into submission.
I, not knowing what was to befall me.

Now I understand. I blossomed too quickly.
I entered your secret room blindfolded,
Feeling your young breasts tenderly
And touching the shape of your limbs.

I suggested we float to the floor
Or ceiling, and enjoy sweetly
The fruits of this mystery.
I, who had never known another.

The room, with its unfamiliar scents
And window open on the future to come,
Comforted my wonderment and awe.
And, by the way, cradled my innocence.

All rooms have a necessary exit.
Silly me, to give my love so carelessly,
As I look back now, unblindfolded,
And armored with wise protection.

I reflect on that room, in quiet moments,
And of course, on you, who went on
To suck precious love from others.

By the way, the room is empty now,
And the window barred.

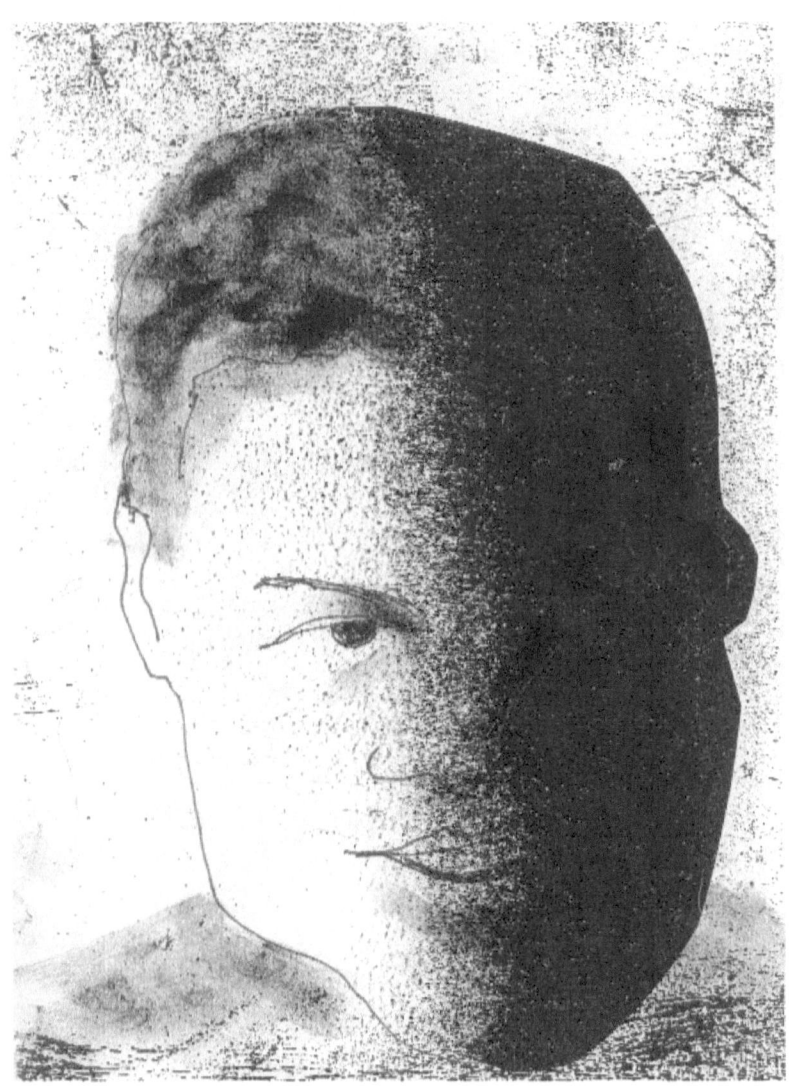

THE END

When the cinema usher
Motions that I exit with the others
As the final credits appear
On the screen of my life
And the swollen music
Has dwindled to its departing chords,
I will stretch my legs and arms
From having dwelled too long
Among empty popcorn cups
In the saga of some celluloid martyr
Who captured, lost, courted, married
The perfect match to his life,
And then went on, like me
To take one last step up to the stage
And disappear beyond the curtain.
Into the Looking Glass House.

www.ingramcontent.com/pod-product-compliance
Lightning Source LLC
Chambersburg PA
CBHW020535060726
47499CB00017B/125